To dear

Caribbean
Adventure

A NOVEL

BY DR. GRACE ALLMAN BURKE

Happy Reading!
Grace Burke
Oct/07/18

Requests for permission to make copies of any part of the work, or to order, should be mailed to the author at Post Office Box 113274, Carrollton, Texas, 75011 or emailed to www.graceaburke.com.

ISBN-13: 978-1475295641

ISBN-10: 1475295642

LCCN: 2012908194
Createspace, N. Charleston, SC

Endorsements

"Grace Allman Burke captures the pulse and flavor of the Caribbean Islands in a fresh and exciting way. Although it's a fictional work, the places visited and travel experiences of the main characters are quite authentic."

– Badonna Birdsong, Travel Agent, Dallas, Texas

"As a native West Indian, I thoroughly enjoyed taking this fast-paced junket through the islands in the pages of *Caribbean Adventure*. Young readers will be filled with anticipation at the prospect of visiting our area of the world."

– Shelley Miller, Marketing and Sales,
Barbados West Indies

"*Caribbean Adventure* was fun to read and made us feel very prepared for our next trip to the West Indies. Even though we'd been to a few of the islands before, we learned a lot of new things, which will help us enjoy ourselves even more."

– Gavrie E. and Nailah E., young travelers,
Mt. Kisco, New York

"Grace has deftly combined loads of fun with an in-depth educational experience in this 'must read' for young people."

– Patricia Brome, Retired Banker and Frequent Tourist,
Savannah, Georgia

In Memory of
My Beloved Goddaughter Amanda

Table of Contents

Acknowlegements

Grateful appreciation is expressed to Oliver Brome, Pauline Russell-Brown, Enid Carter, Angela Cropper, and Sabina Francis, all of whom in various ways contributed to the development of this book. Special thanks and tribute are also paid to the late Keith Allman, Carolyn Barrow, and Helen McDowell, who provided information, wonderful ideas, and encouragement and who now have passed on. Credit is expressed to Amanda Rivers, my deceased god-daughter, who had granted me permission to use her name as the main character of this book. Although she did not live to see its publication, the book is dedicated to her memory. I owe a debt of gratitude to Brooks LaTouche Photographers, the Barbados Government Information Service, and the late Leonard Higginson for photographs used, by permission, in this book.

Thanks to Willis Davis who capably created the cover for this book.

Most of all, my deepest thanks are expressed to my husband, Neville, for his patience and loyal support throughout the writing of this book, and to my children, Cran, Jhan, and Ji, my biggest fan club.

Prologue

One lazy summer afternoon, Amanda Rivers, now a grown woman of 40, is sitting on the sun porch of her large, brick- and- stone, Tudor-style home on New York's Long Island, waiting for her husband and three children to return from the beach. While waiting, she reflects on an amazing time in her life as a teenager. It was 1979 when she took a journey of a lifetime to the Caribbean islands. It was such an exciting and memorable experience for her that she vowed to return there someday. Now, many years later, the time to fulfill that promise has come, and, soon, she'll be taking her own family on a luxury cruise to the islands.

Amanda vividly remembers every detail of that trip, but she hasn't shared a lot about it with her family up to this time. However, now that they're about to embark on their own adventure, she wants to whet their appetites and prepare them to experience the delights of that part of the world. She closes her eyes and thinks back about her various island explorations and decides what she'll tell them before they go……

CHAPTER 1

All Aboard!

Fourteen-year-old Mandy felt transported as she eagerly leafed through the travel brochure. Her aunt Joyce had mailed it to her and she read through it almost every night in bed before falling to sleep.

"Come with us on a fascinating journey to some tropical isles," it invited. "Pick an island of your dreams. Hear the gentle music of sea, sand, and sun. Feel the splash of tiny waves against soft, sugary sand. Hear the whisper of the sea breezes rustling in the palm trees. View the beach, gleaming white in pure tropical sunlight, the air warm and sweet."

She closed her eyes and pictured herself there already.

"It sounds like paradise," she mused.

Ever since Aunt Joyce had invited her to visit the Caribbean, Mandy had thought of little else. How she longed to be on her way to experience the islands with her favorite aunt! She looked forward to meeting some relatives and several of Aunt Joyce's friends along the way, as well.

Mandy, tall, confident, and outspoken, was quite mature for her years. Her infectious laugh and zest for living made others easily gravitate toward her. Lithe and lively, her parents told her that she must have inherited her adventurous spirit from her youthful aunt, herself a roving nomad!

Joyce was an attractive flight attendant who had moved from New York to Barbados, an eastern Caribbean island, three years earlier. Her dark brown, flawless skin blended well with the starched, white uniform that she wore while at work. Her easy-going, friendly manner made her well-liked by travelers, and her co-workers. She adored her niece, Amanda, and, whenever she made a brief stopover in New York on her flights from the Caribbean, she was sure to call Mandy to chat with her and exchange the latest news about family and friends. This made Mandy feel so "of age" in her company.

Mandy continued reading the colorful travel brochure:

"These sun-splashed gems in the Caribbean Sea are bubbling with excitement and adventure," she read. "We'll view cascading waterfalls in Ocho Rios and sight sea urchins in the Bucco Reef. We'll ride the rapids of the Rio Grande and climb to the ancient citadel in Cap Haitien. So hurry! Climb aboard! You'll never be the same."

Mandy could hardly wait until school was out for the summer and her island adventure would begin. In just a few more days, Mandy would fly from New York and meet her aunt in Miami. From there, over the next eight weeks, they would travel leisurely from island to island by plane.

Mandy's grandparents had immigrated to the United States long ago from the Caribbean. They had often spoken about their childhood days in the "British West Indies," as they called them. Mandy had always yearned to visit these places, and now her dream was about to come true.

The local librarian had become a real friend to Mandy over the past few months, helping Mandy learn as much as possible about the Caribbean region prior to her trip. One book that Mandy read described the wide geographical region that the islands cover:

"Beginning off the coast of Florida, the islands stretch southerly, forming a winding chain, broken by the shining blue waters of the Caribbean Sea and ending close to the beautiful country of Venezuela on the continent of South America."

As Mandy glanced at the back of the travel brochure, which showed a map of the West Indies, she marked the places she and her aunt would tour with a bright red marker. Their first stop would be Nassau in the Bahamas—a forty-five-minute jet hop from Miami. Their journey would then take them zigzagging through the island chain until they reached their final destination of Curaçao.

At dinner that evening, Mandy talked about her trip with her family. "We're going to ten different islands!" she chattered excitedly to her brother, Matthew. "I wish you'd hurry up and go," he answered, exasperated. "That's all you ever talk about these days."

Mandy grinned tolerantly at her younger brother. "You're just jealous, Matt. You know you'd give your right arm to be going with us."

"All right, you two," their mom, Margaret, intervened, chuckling. "Be sure to send us a postcard from every place you visit, Mandy. I know you'll have a grand time with Joyce and her friends. My sister has always been a live wire."

While her family was certainly excited for her, Mandy was the absolute envy of her friends. Her best friend, Diane, who lived in the house next door, kept telling her how lucky she was to have an aunt like Joyce. And Carl, who Mandy referred to as her "closest guy friend," told her how much he'd miss her and even said that if she didn't hurry back, then he might just have to fly down and get her himself.

As Mandy packed that night for her trip, she remembered what Joyce had advised about packing lightly since they would be so much on the go. She glanced again at the letter from her aunt, just as she'd done a thousand times already in the weeks before. "The dress down here is mainly casual," her aunt had written. "But throw in one or two fancy items. We might just get invited to some dazzling evening affairs!" Her aunt continued, "Don't forget to bring along your folding umbrella. The showers never last long, but our summer cloudbursts can be drenching at times."

Finally, the day of departure arrived. Mandy hardly noticed the familiar hustling and bustling of New York as she drove from Manhattan to the airport for her dream flight southward.

"Did you remember to bring your passport, dear?" her father inquired as they approached the terminal.

"How could I forget, Dad?" she replied. "This will be my first time outside of the country, remember?"

Upon arriving at the airport, Mandy confidently checked her bags and then turned, waving to the group of well-wishers who'd gathered to see her off. Upon hearing the boarding call, Mandy stepped smartly up the ramp to get on the aircraft, settling her slender frame comfortably into her wide-cushioned seat. Humming a catchy, popular tune softly to herself, she could almost taste, hear, and feel the pulsating rhythms from those distant islands as they beckoned her.

Smiling contentedly, she whispered in reply, "Caribbean, here I come!"

CHAPTER 2

Breezy Bahamas

"We have just landed on New Providence Island, ladies and gentlemen," came the lilting, almost musical voice of the flight attendant. "Nassau, the capital city of the Bahamas, is located here. Kindly take all hand luggage with you, and thanks for flying with us."

Mandy was certain that the other passengers could hear her heart pounding as she and her aunt prepared to exit from the airplane.

"We're here, Aunt Joyce," she whispered excitedly. "I can't believe we're really here!"

Mandy and her aunt had had a joyful reunion in Miami. They'd chatted incessantly while waiting for their Nassau-bound plane to depart. Now, at last, their long-awaited Caribbean adventure had begun.

"Is everything so formal here?" Mandy asked her aunt quietly as they passed through immigration and customs. The crisp, serious manner of the impeccably-dressed officers was rather unexpected.

"It can be quite formal at times," Joyce hastened to explain. "The starchy, rather conservative approach is probably a carryover from the British influence when many of these islands were colonies. But, you'll soon see that the relaxed and casual manner of the people you meet is quite the opposite."

Mandy gazed out of the window of the taxicab as they drove through the narrow, winding streets toward their hotel. The brilliant rays of the noonday sun cast shadows through the branches of giant coconut palms. Tropical flowers of many hues were everywhere. Children darted here and there. Women bustled toward the marketplace. The sights, sounds, and smells were a delightfully new experience for her.

Once settled into their hotel, Mandy and Joyce sat relaxing on the balcony of their room, inhaling the refreshingly clean aroma of the salty ocean breeze. The crystal clear water ranged in shade from emerald to pale aquamarine to regal blue.

"No wonder you enjoy living down here," declared Mandy to her aunt. "If I were you, I'd never want to move back to the ice and snow of cold New York."

Joyce, laughing, replied, "You're right. I love the tropical climate and friendly lifestyle here. But, I miss the change of seasons back home. It's easy to lose track of the time of year in this part of the world where the temperature varies so little."

Dinner that night was a grand occasion. A sumptuous buffet was served under the stars. The evening was called

"Buccaneer Night," reminiscent of the Bahamas' history of pirates and buccaneers in centuries past.

"Good evening, Madame and young lady," greeted the congenial, silver-haired maitre d'hôtel. As he ushered them courteously to seats in the dining area, he inquired, "Is this your first visit to the Bahamas?"

"My aunt has been here before," replied Mandy. "But this is my first time."

"Well, enjoy every minute of it," he urged, "and be sure to visit the Family Islands, also, while you're here."

Mandy had read before coming on their trip that the nation of the Bahamas is actually a group of over 700 islands and 3,000 rocks and cays in the Atlantic Ocean. They stretch nearly 500 miles, although relatively few of them are inhabited. The Family Islands, with exotic names like Bimini and Eleuthra, among others, form a necklace of settlements, famous for their beaches, fishing, and easy-going atmosphere.

"Will we be visiting the Family Islands?" Mandy inquired of Joyce when they were seated.

"I'm not sure that we'll have time," she replied. "Jean and Dorothy are coming over tomorrow to take us shopping. By the time we get around Nassau and visit Paradise Island, too, it will be time to take off for Jamaica. But, we'll see. Right now, though, I'm starving. Let's get something to eat."

The heavily-laden buffet table was truly a connoisseur's delight. There was a great variety of mouthwatering delicacies harvested from the surrounding seas. Lobster salad, conch fritters, and crab croquettes were served with rich, spicy sauces. Heaping platters of pork and beef were marinated to Bahamian perfection. Steaming cauldrons of stews and vegetables were present in abundance.

"My clothes won't fit by the end of this trip," Mandy lamented as she savored the last morsel of her rich dessert. "I don't think I've ever eaten so much in all my life."

"Be sure to take a book of West Indian cooking back home with you," her aunt advised. "Each island has its own national dishes and delightful blends of seasonings and spices."

By ten o'clock the next morning, Bay Street was already teeming with tourists. Dorothy and Jean, Joyce's Bahamian friends, had arrived early to pick them up.

"Three cruise ships are in port today," Dot informed them. "We normally have a lot of visitors, but when the liners come in, it's really congested."

"It reminds me of downtown New York!" Mandy exclaimed. "But the air is cleaner and it's sunnier and brighter here," she hastened to add with a wink.

"This section is the hub of Nassau's business district," Jean told them. "Whatever you're looking for, you'll find it here on Bay Street."

Mandy was intrigued as they strolled past stores of all descriptions. Many sold crystal, jewelry, perfume, and other merchandise from around the world. They were displayed in modern, tastefully-decorated shop windows. Between were vendors' stalls containing items ranging from straw goods to foodstuff.

Mandy browsed through some of the local handicraft. Baskets, handbags, placemats, even briefcases intricately braided from straw, were on sale. She selected a wide-brimmed sun hat for herself and picked out a few postcards and souvenirs for her family and friends back home.

"Watch your pennies," Joyce reminded her gently. "We still have many more places to visit."

"I'll be careful," Mandy agreed good-naturedly. "It's hard to resist not buying everything in sight!"

When they finished their shopping expedition, the foursome took a lunch break in an elegant downtown restaurant. Then, they moved across town to visit some other places of interest.

Their companions-cum-tour guides took them crisscrossing through the tiny, quaint streets. They were shown the courthouse, the main post office, and the House of Assembly on Rawson Square where the government's official business is conducted.

Mandy was impressed by Government House—a solid, handsome mansion where the Governor General resides. A while marble statue of Christopher Columbus stood outside. She learned that the statue was erected there in Columbus' honor because he landed, first, in the Bahamas upon his arrival in the New World in 1492.

Their final stop was the famous Queen's Staircase, one of the city's biggest tourist attractions. As they navigated briskly up its sixty-six steps, Jean advised them that each step commemorated a year of Queen Victoria's reign. Once at the top, they viewed the city and surrounding areas from the water tower.

Footsore and exhausted, Mandy and Joyce returned to their hotel in the late afternoon after bidding goodbye to Jean and Dot, feeling that their day had indeed been well spent.

The last stint of their three-day Bahamian sojourn was a leisurely day on Paradise Island—a celebrated cove connected to Nassau by a toll bridge—where they relaxed completely on the lovely beach. While there, Joyce donned her snorkeling mask to view the wonders beneath the briny deep. After splashing around in the warm, gentle waves, Mandy combed the beach, collecting shells of various sizes and shapes. A while later, they collapsed in their beach chairs, soaking up the glorious sunshine.

"Tomorrow we're Jamaica bound," murmured Joyce, half-sleepily.

"Is it anything like Nassau?" Mandy inquired.

"Oh no," Joyce replied. "Although the islands have much in common, each is quite unique. Jamaica is much larger, so there's much more to see and do."

"I'm really looking forward to going there," Mandy declared. "I enjoyed the Bahamas, but the waterfalls and mountains in Jamaica that I read about sound really exciting."

"It's great being a tourist for a change," said her aunt. "My job rarely affords me the opportunity of seeing more than airports and hotels on my brief stopovers. Visiting the countryside in Jamaica will be a wonderful change."

That night as they stood on their balcony, Mandy sighed breathlessly and whispered to Joyce, "God really smiled on these islands."

The sky was a panorama of stars, and the full, tropical moon hung low, sending shafts of silvery light across the shimmering ocean waves.

Joyce agreed, "The tall buildings and bright lights of the cities up North hide these wonders of creation."

"I feel like staying in this spot forever," Mandy languidly said.

"Nine more islands to go, kiddo," said Joyce, pleasantly shifting the mood. "And it gets better as we go."

The tropical moonlight sends shafts of silvery
light across shimmering ocean waves.
Photo by Leonard Higginson, New York, N.Y.

CHAPTER 3

Jaunt Through Jamaica

"Good morning, Jamaica!" Mandy exclaimed as she glanced around at the lush vegetation.

The quiet dawn screamed in silent reply as she wandered through the cool gardens, waiting for her host and hostess to awaken. After bidding farewell to their Bahamian friends, Mandy and Joyce winged their way southwesterly to this land of dazzling beauty. Here, they were staying with their cousins, Blossom and Freddy, a charming couple whose home was nestled in the heart of Jamaica's famous Blue Mountains. Mandy learned that the flavorful coffee from the plantations that dotted the mountain range made its way to many ports around the world. This was the second day of their visit to this magnificent island, a sparkling gem in the Greater Antilles.

Mandy tried to imagine what life might have been like here for Quashiba Rowe, her great-grandmother, many years ago. Born in Jamaica in the northern parish of St. Elizabeth, Mandy's great-grandmother was raised in

Kingston, the capital. She left the island as a young woman in the early part of the twentieth century, joining thousands of other West Indians on their trek to Panama for the construction of the Canal. She later returned to Jamaica where she raised her family. Many years later, she immigrated to the US. As a child, Mandy had listened with rapt attention as the old lady spun tales for her of Jamaica's rich history. She told of Maroons leading slave revolts, and Port Royal, then called "Sin City," and many other adventures as she described the island's colorful past.

"Up so soon?" came a husky voice behind her.

Startled, Mandy turned to find Freddy ready for work in his garden. He was pleased that he'd done his own landscaping. The neatly manicured lawn and the even shrubs and flowering bushes all resulted from his labor. Hibiscus, crotons, anthuriums, and oleanders were clustered around its edges. A tree bearing the national flower, the lignum vitae, was there displaying its lovely blue petals.

"It's so peaceful here," Mandy replied. "I couldn't resist a morning stroll."

"It's great to be on vacation, isn't it?" Freddy declared.

During the school year, Freddy was a lecturer at the University of the West Indies, a regional institution. Mandy learned that its main campus in Jamaica attracts students from throughout the Caribbean. Many of the teachers, lawyers, and other professionals who practice in the islands are graduates of its programs.

Back at the house, Blossom and Joyce were chatting away when Mandy entered the kitchen. The hearty breakfast, typical of Jamaica, included ackee and saltfish, fried dumplings, and green bananas. It was delicious and kept her satisfied for the rest of the day.

"Are you ready for the trip to Port Antonio today?" Joyce asked her with a twinkle. She knew that Mandy had really been looking forward to it.

"You bet," she excitedly replied. "I can't wait to get aboard that raft!"

They traveled by car to Port Antonio, a town of old-world charm. As they approached the river, several bamboo rafts came into view. Each accommodated two passengers, piloted by a local raftsman. Freddy and Blossom boarded one while Joyce and Mandy boarded another.

They were guided expertly on their seven-mile cruise down the expansive Rio Grande. From its brisk beginning to its placid ending, the two-and-a-half hour voyage was truly an escapade. The raftsmen called to each other in "Jamaica talk," the local dialect, also called Patois.

"Ello. Wha' appen?" said one, translated, " Hi, what's up?"

The other answered, "Mi woud radda yu nuh chat to me," translated, "I would rather you not talk to me."

Mandy understood very little of it, especially since it was spoken so quickly. But she was fascinated by its harsh and rapid sound.

Navigating along the winding river, the scenic beauty captivated them. As they rode through the rapids, negotiating the bends and viewing the tropical flora along the river banks, Mandy felt blessed to have experienced such a meeting with nature. Their delightful caper ended downstream where the river joined the sea at St. Margaret's Bay.

"I'm famished!" Blossom exclaimed as they returned to the car.

"How about some jerk pork?" suggested Freddy. "This parish of Portland is the place for it, you know."

"What's jerk pork?" Mandy questioned.

"It's our local style of roasting pork over an open fire," he explained. "It's something like barbecuing."

"Sounds good," declared Mandy. "I'd like to try it."

"Is it spicy?" Joyce asked.

"It certainly is. I'm sure you'll like it."

They stopped the car by a group of wayside vendors. Jerk pork was their specialty. It was hot and steaming with a mouthwatering fragrance.

Freddy bought some coconuts from another vendor nearby, who had several on a large open cart. He chopped off the tops of the thick green fruit.

"No need for glasses," he laughed, as he took a long deep drink of the flavorful cool water inside.

After thoroughly enjoying their meal, the four then proceeded homeward.

The following day, Blossom introduced Mandy to Lena, Sam, and Louis, young friends of theirs who lived in the bustling city of Kingston. For the rest of her weeklong stay on the island, Mandy was inseparable from this trio. She felt completely at home with them, and they showed her Jamaica from many dimensions. She gleaned from them first hand what life was like for young people in the Caribbean, realizing at the same time how very different an island upbringing is from her own childhood growing up in a large metropolitan city.

The foursome set off for a day in town, leaving Joyce relaxing at home with Blossom and Freddy. Their first stop was a local market, which proved to be quite an experience for Mandy. The place was a beehive of activity as women referred to as "higglers" called to passersby. Seated behind wide wooden trays and baskets, the higglers weighed the fruit and vegetables on portable scales. The women wore gaily-colored head wraps, and their large-pocketed aprons jingled with coins. Deftly, they supplied change to their customers who handed them currency notes.

Louis, a tall handsome fellow, was well known around this market. A friendly chat with his favorite higgler resulted in some free mangoes for them to eat as they strolled along. The pulpy, yellow, succulent fruit tasted delightful to Mandy. The friends pointed out other tropical produce to Mandy as well. Soursop and star apple were there for sale. Mandy noticed that soursop, a little larger in size than a grapefruit, has a dark-green, prickly skin. The inside is creamy white, with small, black seeds. Lena explained that soursop can be made into a delicious drink, as well as ice cream, and, it also has various medicinal uses. She said that many elderly people believe that it's good for high blood pressure and other ailments. Its name in Spanish is guanabana. When her friends pointed out the star apples, Mandy saw that these fruit were purple and green-colored on both the inside and outside. She was intrigued by the lovely star pattern it displayed when this fruit was cut in half.

Mandy also learned about several vegetables that were unfamiliar to her. Among them were plantains, which look like bananas, only larger, and breadfruit, which has a thick, green skin and grows on tall, full-leafed trees.

"Let's stop at 'Mama T's' for lunch," Lena later proposed.

"Good idea," agreed Sam as they exited from the market. "Her place is just up the road a little."

Mama T, a buxom, cheerful middle-aged woman was renowned in Kingston for her excellent cooking. Her huge pots bubbled at the rear of her small, intimate restaurant, emanating rich aromas of native Jamaican dishes.

"Hello there, Mama T," called Sam. "Meet our American friend, Mandy. This is her first time here."

Mama T flashed a smile and welcomed Mandy warmly. Her large gold-hooped earrings glinted in the brilliant sunlight that filtered in.

"What's cooking today?" Lena inquired.

"The curry goat is fine," she replied. "The patties are ready, too."

While there, the place grew crowded with noontime customers. They ate heartily and washed their meal down with ginger beer, a pungent, refreshing beverage, very popular in Jamaica.

Boarding a bus afterward, they traveled to Sabina Park to spend the afternoon at a cricket match. The enthusiastic crowd was deeply engrossed in the play. "This is one of our national sports," Louis informed Mandy. "It's somewhat like your baseball. See if you can follow it."

Children playing a game of cricket—the
favorite national sport of the islands.
Photo by Leonard Higginson, New York, N.Y.

Mandy heard unfamiliar terms like "wicket-keeper," "bowler," and "batsman" as the game progressed.

"If my stay here were longer, I'm sure I'd get to understand it," she promised. "But it's fun to watch anyway."

Glancing around, she was surprised at the cosmopolitan nature of the local crowd.

"I didn't realize that there were so many other races and cultures in Jamaica," she commented. "I thought most West Indians were of African descent."

"The majority of our people are," Sam explained. "But we also have many Chinese, Indians, and Syrians in our country."

Lena, a lover of history, elaborated further. "The original inhabitants of Jamaica were Arawak Indians. The first Europeans, the Spaniards, arrived much later in the fifteenth century. About two hundred years afterward, our African forefathers were brought here as slaves, then later emancipated. The British settled here in the late 1600s after battles with the Spanish. The Asians came as indentured servants, while the Lebanese and Syrians followed more recently."

"Very interesting," Mandy replied. "And who are those fellows over there with the dreadlock braids in their hair?

"They are Rastafarians," replied Sam. "We call them 'Rastas' for short. They are members of a religious sect that engages in the mystical worship of Haile Selassie, former Emperor of Ethiopia."

Mandy was fascinated by this.

"Their hair and style of dress are their symbols," Lena interjected. "They have certain dietary rules as well."

"Did you hear that catchy Reggae music that was playing when we passed the record shops in town?" asked Sam. "The Rastas play it often. You hear it all over Jamaica and in the other islands as well."

"Yes, I recognized it. It's played a lot in New York also," said Mandy.

Very proud of his country, Louis stoutly averred, "Although our various groups practice their own religions and customs, we are all thoroughly Jamaican."

The most unforgettable part of her stay in the island was Mandy's visit to its north coast. Joyce was as anxious as she was to get there.

"You can't appreciate the trip unless you spend at least two days there," Blossom had advised. "Some friends of ours, Lela and Ernest, have a villa near the seaside. We've been promising them a visit for a long time. I know they'll be delighted to have us overnight with them."

At the crack of dawn, the two-car caravan set out. Freddy, with Blossom and Lena, led the way. Joyce drove behind, carrying Mandy, Sam, and Louis, her rollicking passengers. They were heading for Ocho Rios in the parish of St. Ann. It's called the "garden parish," and Mandy soon discovered why. The sixty-mile journey took them over hills and valleys, past rich, fertile fields and plains. Huge herds of cattle grazed in shady green pastures. Vast acres of sugar cane, cocoa, bananas, and the pimento spice portrayed Jamaica at its rural best. Halfway there, the roving band stopped at the town of Ewarton, which has a bauxite mining plant.

"Bauxite is a mineral ore from which aluminum is manufactured," Freddy explained. "It's one of our most important natural resources."

Joyce and Mandy noticed that the mining of this product is a vast operation.

Lena pointed to the rust-colored soil underfoot. "This is our famous red earth from which the bauxite comes. After it is mined, it is exported to many countries of the world. The US is one of our biggest customers."

"So you see, my dear girl," Sam jested, "although you didn't know it, you've been introduced to Jamaica already."

Mandy wrinkled her brow at him quizzically.

"Think of all of the things back home that are made from aluminum," he explained. "Your car engines, airplanes, buckets, basins, and one-thousand-one other items. Who knows? Even the pots and pans in your kitchen may have originated from this very spot."

Mandy winked at him good naturedly when he had finished speaking. "When I get back home, whenever I cook, I'll always remember our talk, Sam," she promised.

Several miles further, they passed through Fern Gully on the outskirts of Ocho Rios. Driving downhill, they meandered slowly along the three-mile stretch of road. Mandy was enchanted by the many varieties of tropical ferns that grew wildly in the area. Overhanging hardwood trees formed a cool, tunnel-like path, which nearly hid the sunlight of the lovely valley.

About noon, approximately two miles beyond Fern Gully, they arrived at the world-famous Dunn's River Falls. Mandy learned that this national treasure of Jamaica is a "must do" activity for everyone visiting this island. She soon discovered that it's a major Caribbean tourist attraction, for, when they arrived, she noticed that scores of people had already converged on the area. Blossom and Freddy had advised them to wear sturdy shoes and to bring along a waterproof camera for picture-taking. Donning their bathing suits, they entered a stretch of beach, and, Mandy observed that people of all ages were there to experience the exciting climb up the Falls. High above them and beside them, several cool mountain streams cascaded downward, covering them with their glistening foam. They flowed gently, then more swiftly over jagged rocks and boulders, merging at last with the warm Caribbean Sea below.

A local tour guide assisted Sam and Louis in leading their party up the steep ascent. Mandy and Lena were close behind at first, holding hands to help keep each other balanced. But they later slowed down to rest and swim in one of the plateau-like lagoons. Joyce trod determinedly but cautiously after nearly losing her footing at one point, as Freddy and Blossom brought up the rear.

Puffing, laughing, and panting after the one and one-half-hour's climb, they all finally made it up the 600-foot-high precipice. They chatted a while on the cool mountaintop, bought crafts and souvenirs on sale there, and posed for breathtaking photos. It seemed as if the much easier trek downward didn't take nearly as long as the hike upward.

When dressed again like civilians, they ate ravenously afterward at a nearby restaurant, and, all concluded that coming to this celebrated nature spot had been well worth the trip. The rest of the afternoon was spent perusing the shops in the town of Ocho Rios, the second largest tourist resort in Jamaica. As dusk approached, they arrived at the home of their friends, who eagerly awaited them. The cozy, immaculate villa was found at the end of a winding road. It sat snugly in a narrow cove on the shores of a white, sandy beach.

Ernest hurried down the marble staircase to meet them. He was gray-haired and distinguished-looking and puffed on an ochre-colored pipe.

"Lela, they're here!" he called behind him. "Welcome, welcome," he greeted in a deep, resonant Jamaican accent. "Go right inside. Make yourselves comfortable."

A diminutive but vivacious woman appeared. "So you've reached at last!" Lela exclaimed, hugging each one. Kiddingly, she chided Blossom and Freddy, "So it took a visit from your American cousins to finally get you here!"

Passing through a cool, shady courtyard, they entered a room filled with memorabilia. There were woven rugs and tapestries, leatherwork, wooden figurines, masks, and vases.

An indoor garden of hanging baskets, ferns, and flowering plants tastefully completed its décor.

Lela and Ernest were retired after having lived many years in West Africa. Jamaican by birth, they had returned home last year, settling into this restful seafront hideaway.

"This is marvelous!" Joyce exclaimed, grateful for the comfort of a lounge chair after their action-packed day. The young people explored the villa while the older ones exchanged their own bits of news. After feasting on the scrumptious dinner that Lela prepared, they retired early, sleeping restfully.

Mandy awakened to the sound of gentle, lapping waves on the secluded beach. She spent the morning enjoying the marvelous ocean all by herself.

After their visit with Lela and Ernest, the final leg of their stay in that part of the island was a visit to the town of St. Ann's Bay, the capital of St. Ann parish. Mandy had requested this brief detour before returning to Blossom and Freddy's place. She wanted to view the statue of Marcus Garvey located there. St. Ann's Bay, seven miles west of Ocho Rios, was the birthplace of Marcus Garvey, one of Jamaica's national heroes.

Mandy was thrilled to see the statue. She had heard and read a lot about this dedicated, dynamic leader who had founded the famous Universal Negro Improvement Association in the 1920s. Its aims had been to improve the conditions of African people all over the world and to unify them toward a common purpose. Garvey had captained the steamship line called the "Black Star," which had sailed several times to West Africa. Its point of departure was Harlem, where New York's largest Black community was located. After viewing the statue, Mandy decided that she would write about Marcus Garvey as the topic of her project in the upcoming school term.

"This week has certainly flown by," declared Joyce the next day as they packed to leave the island.

"I wish the boys and Lena could come with us on the rest of our tour," said Mandy sadly. She realized that she'd made some lifelong friends.

They were all at the airport to see Mandy and Joyce off as the duo proceeded to their next port of call, Haiti. The doors of the big jet closed. The captain revved the engines. The aircraft began its ascent. Mandy smiled with great anticipation as she wondered what lay in store for them when they reached that mysterious isle.

CHAPTER 4

Haitian Holiday

Joyce and Mandy heard their names being called as they emerged from the busy airport. Billie Mills, Joyce's American friend, hurried toward them.

"Billie, how good to see you!" cried Joyce.

"You've made your first trip to Haiti at last!" she replied, as they embraced warmly.

Joyce and Billie had been college roommates and had remained close friends over the years. They hadn't seen each other for quite some time, although they corresponded often.

"You must be Mandy," Billie said. "I've heard so much about you."

Joyce quickly introduced them and declared, "I'm so excited to be here!"

Billie had been assigned to Haiti for the past five years by the international agency for which she worked.

Mandy knew that this French-speaking country occupied a portion of the island of Hispaniola. The other part of the island comprised the Spanish-speaking nation of the Dominican Republic and was different from it in every respect.

Mandy listened attentively as Billie addressed her chauffeur in fluent French. She understood a little of what was said since she'd studied beginning French at school.

She could hardly believe that they were receiving such noble service as Monsieur Moreau escorted them to the official car. He bowed courteously and signaled them to enter as he opened the door. They traveled through the streets of Port-au-Prince, the densely populated capital city, and soon were on their way to Pétionville where Billie lived. Mandy stared in amazement as they whisked past teeming masses of people. The movement, the noises, the colors were dizzying to the senses. They had truly entered a different world.

"I really feel like a foreigner now," she remarked quietly to Joyce. "This is nothing like Jamaica or the Bahamas. The people look West Indian, but they're all speaking French."

"Actually, what you're hearing is Creole," Billie advised.

"How is Creole different from French?" Joyce inquired.

"French is the official language of Haiti. It is taught in the schools and is spoken on formal occasions. Creole, which most people speak, is a dialect in which African, Spanish, and English words have been added to the French. A French-speaking person can understand Creole if it is spoken slowly."

They cautiously traversed the narrow road that curved upward and led to the elite suburb of Pétionville. The road was lined on either side with humanity in every form. Graceful market women bearing loads on their heads wended to and from Port-au-Prince. Artists displayed their paintings and leather goods by the roadside. Brightly-decorated, painted pickup trucks continuously tooted their horns, and were overflowing with people and produce. They were among the main contributors to the bustling traffic.

"Those are called 'Tap-taps,' our local passenger vans," Billie informed them.

"Why are they named 'Tap-taps?'" Mandy asked.

Billie chuckled and answered, "When passengers in the vans want the drivers to stop so that they can exit, they tap the side of the van. Hence, the name, 'Tap-tap.'"

As they arrived in Pétionville, Mandy noticed that the shady, tree-lined streets in the area were in sharp contrast to the hot and dusty rutted roads they'd left behind. Handsome villas, reminiscent of Haiti's illustrious past, flaunted the artistic nature of this, the world's first Black republic. Posh restaurants, fancy boutiques, salons de coiffure, discos, and casinos were the hallmarks of the area, home of the country's middle class.

At last they reached Place St. Pierre. The picturesque setting of this lovely village square exuded a feeling of tranquility. The flamboyant trees with their blazing orange blossoms were bursting fully into bloom. Stately cypress firs guarded each corner of the square. Église St. Pierre, with its arched stained-glass windows and white coral stone façade, stood in elegant beauty on one side facing the square. Its ever-open doorway invited worshippers and visitors alike to enter.

Billie lived in an expansive apartment overlooking the square. Its decorative wrought-iron grilled balcony afforded a marvelous view of the rolling hillside in the distance. From this vantage point, she could take note of all that transpired in three different directions.

"I've attended extravagant weddings and modest funerals from my terrace," Billie remarked with a laugh. "It's as if I receive a special invitation to major events of the quartier."

Mr. Moreau deposited their luggage in Billie's apartment. After that she discharged him, deciding to drive her own car for the rest of the weekend.

"Are the shops still open?" Joyce eagerly inquired, glancing at her watch. "I want to feast my eyes on those paintings I've heard so much about."

"You haven't changed a bit, Joyce," Billie responded. "Always on the move. Yes, they're open until late since it's Friday. How about you, Mandy? Do you feel like going now?"

"That's fine with me," Mandy replied. "The weekend will be over before we know it, so we might as well take advantage of every minute."

Billie maneuvered her car deftly through the maze of roads and soon arrived on the outskirts of Port-au-Prince. Swinging into a quiet, narrow street, she parked outside an ornate three-storied building. Mandy observed that it resembled an old restored mansion. It had high wooden shutters and louvered windows. Each tier contained a separate balcony encircled by an intricately-carved iron railing. A flowered pathway led them to a locked marble door. A connecting path continued to the gardens beyond. A nearly faded sign announced it as a "Galerie d'Art."

The visitors waited with heightened curiosity after Billie pressed the doorbell. After what seemed like an eternity, the entrance finally swung open. Mandy quietly gasped in astonishment as an extremely large, but elegant woman filled the doorway. She was dressed in a flowing boldly-colored print gown. Her feet were shod with surprisingly tiny slippers. Her handsome face bore almond-shaped eyes, and her smooth, velvety skin was the color of mocha chocolate. An array of silver and gold bangles bedecked her arms. Her thick black hair, swept high atop her head, was held in place by decorative lavender combs. They sparkled in the waning afternoon sunlight like jewels on an ebony throne. Her face became wreathed in smiles as she recognized Billie.

"Please, please come in," she invited in halting English.

Billie introduced her to Joyce and Mandy as Madame St. Jacques, a leading fashion designer and dressmaker in the area.

"Please meet my American friends, Madame. They arrived only today in Haiti for a very brief visit."

"It is my pleasure," she replied most politely when they were seated. "But why is your stay so short? There is much of our country to see."

Mandy was charmed by her lovely French accent.

Joyce responded, "We are touring through the islands, Madame. So our time in each place is limited. Someday, though, we promise to return."

Madame St. Jacques smiled broadly. "Well then, enjoy as much of it as you can."

Their portly hostess arose. "May I offer you some tea?" she inquired. "Billie is a special friend of mine, you know."

"We'd love some, Madame," said Mandy.

Madame clapped her hands and a young servant girl appeared. She ordered the refreshments and resumed their conversation.

"Madame has made a number of outfits for me," Billie advised them. "I'm sure she won't mind showing you some of her creations."

"Not at all," she replied, leaving them for a moment.

Joyce glanced at the walls around them. They were lined with paintings of all descriptions—originals by Madame's husband, Henri St. Jacques, a local artist.

Mandy and Joyce perused the canvases, lingering a long time at each one. Through oils and other media, they depicted Haiti's diverse lifestyle. There were highly color-ful market scenes, portraits in charcoal, and land and sea-scapes, not to mention the many religious portrayals of Christianity and voodoo in this highly mystical isle of six million people.

"They are all so magnificent," Joyce declared. "Are any for sale? I'd certainly like to buy some if they are."

Before Billie could respond, the servant reappeared with a tray of steaming tea and delectable biscuits. Madame followed close behind with samples of her handiwork.

"Is Monsieur St. Jacques at home?" inquired Billie. "I think my friend here is captivated by some paintings."

"I'm expecting him momentarily," she replied. "I am sure he will offer you reasonable prices."

While they exchanged pleasantries, Henri St. Jacques arrived.

"Quite the opposite of Madame," Mandy silently observed.

He was extremely slender, of average height, and sported a head full of tight-graying curls. His sharp, angular features and olive complexion bespoke his mixed ancestry. He was rather casually dressed in an open-necked shirt and loosely-fitting trousers. A striped cravat tie added an artistic touch to his attire.

"Henri, you are here!" his wife exclaimed. "Please join us for tea."

It was dusk when they returned to Pétionville after visiting with Madame and Henri. Joyce's arms were bulging with paintings. She'd found three that were irresistible. Mandy was measured for an exquisite garment. Madame promised to finish it by the time she and Joyce were ready to leave.

"In case you're wondering, we're eating out tonight," Billie informed them. "One of Haiti's finest restaurants is walking distance from here. I think you'll like it."

"Sounds great," Joyce responded. "I'm starved."

They showered and dressed in preparation for dinner.

The cool night air was refreshing as they jaunted leisurely to their destination. The pleasant aroma of jasmine blossoms wafted to them. The restaurant afforded them a spectacular view of the city and harbor below. They ate outdoors by candlelight, complete with wine for their dining pleasure. When they looked over the menu, they hardly knew where to begin. Billie helped them sample some typical Haitian dishes to which she had become accustomed since living there. For their appetizers, they tried Haitian Chicken Paté puffs, and Akra, which are fritters made from black-eyed peas. These were so tasty that they nearly filled up on them before ordering their entrées. Joyce suggested that they each order something different for their main dish, and then sample a little from each other's. Billie began by ordering 'Poulet á l'haïtienne', which is chicken in spicy Creole sauce. She explained that Haitians enjoy their food well-seasoned with a "kick of spicy" in it. Joyce had a taste for pork, and ordered 'Griots', a crispy fried pork, which she learned was a dish enjoyed in family meals throughout Haiti.

"I'm open to trying anything," Mandy said to Billie. "Is there something you'd suggest?"

"How about the 'Boeuf á l'haïtienne'?" offered Billie. It's beef with tomatoes and peppers and is really delicious."

Mandy agreed to try it and really enjoyed it.

Billie then ordered a few side dishes to go with their entrées, including 'Diri et djondjon', translated, rice and black mushrooms, and fried plantains (Mandy had enjoyed the plantains that she first sampled in Jamaica). Billie asked for 'Pikliz,' a pickled vegetable condiment, that Mandy and Joyce found out is available in every Haitian household to go with their meals.

Although they felt absolutely stuffed, they gave in when the waiter insisted that they try 'Diri olé,' a Haitian rice pudding, for dessert, and 'Sitronand,' a vanilla-flavored lemonade for their beverage.

As they savored their supper, Mandy inquired about Haiti's history.

"Is it true that Haiti was the first Caribbean island to become independent?"

"That's correct," Billie replied. "Four famous generals, now national heroes, fought for Haiti's independence. The battles took place at the turn of the nineteenth century against the French colonials. Their names were Toussaint L'Ouverture, Jean Jacques Dessalines, Alexandre Pétion and Henri Christophe. Through their efforts, slavery was abolished and Haiti became an independent republic in 1804."

"That's fascinating," Joyce commented. "Despite its long period of independence and its Caribbean location, however, it seems as if the French influence is still very strong."

"Are there many historical sites in Haiti?" questioned Mandy.

"There are several," Billie replied. "In fact, the ruins of two monuments, built by Christophe, can be viewed near Cap Haitien."

"I'd love to see them," Mandy responded with great interest.

"We could drive there on Sunday," Billie advised. "We'd have to start early, though. It's about two hundred miles away."

"That's fine with me," agreed Joyce. "That would give us a chance to see another part of Haiti and really make our visit complete."

"We've done a lot already on our first day here," Mandy declared with a yawn as they made their way home that evening.

The next morning Mandy and Joyce awakened to the tantalizing fragrance of Billie's gourmet breakfast.

"Ready for a day in the town?" inquired their hostess.

"I certainly am," Mandy replied. "I've read about the Iron Market. Will we get a chance to visit there?"

"I wouldn't have you miss it for the world," Billie said. "It's an experience you'll never forget. We call it 'Marché de Fer.'"

Dressed in blue jeans and T-shirts, the threesome embarked on a Saturday of bargain hunting.

Port-au-Prince was teeming with people that morning. Women stood on street corners selling neatly folded cloths of flaming hues. Beggars cried for money. Young street urchins bolted everywhere. The stores and shops were a visitor's paradise. A youth in tattered clothing, who was obviously unwashed, insisted on serving as their guide-cum-protector as they moved along. Unable to shake him, Billie advised him good-naturedly in Creole, "You might as well earn your keep then."

He willingly agreed to carry their packages for them for a small fee as they made their purchases.

Joyce selected some delicate jewelry for relatives in New York, which Mandy promised to deliver safely for her. At last, Billie found the distinctive perfume for which she'd long been searching. They perambulated to the other end of town and crossed the Grand Rue.

When they entered Marché de Fer, Mandy discovered that what Billie had told them that morning was no exaggeration. Nothing she had seen thus far on their two-week journey in any way surpassed this. As they thronged through the gateway, they were pushed and prodded by the swirling, sweating mob. Their speech and clothing betrayed them as visitors, and vendors instantly besieged them, loudly inviting them to purchase their wares.

Mandy was uncertain where and how to proceed. It had to be the largest indoor market in the world. Every stall, it seemed, was lined with wall hangings, statues, drums, and masks. There were leather goods, foodstuff, ironwork, and woodcuts galore. The howling of the peddlers was totally unreal.

"This is stupendous!" cried Joyce. "Never in all my life!"

But Mandy was most intrigued by the performance Billie gave. She watched with rapt attention at Billie's mastery of the art of haggling with the vendors. Her accompanying gestures and facial expressions were extremely funny. When a vendor charged a price for an item that Billie thought was too expensive, Billie pretended as if she no longer wanted it and slowly walked away. Of course, the vendor really wanted to make a sale, and lowered the price a little bit. But Billie kept on walking. The vendor, now desperate, called after Billie to come back, and lowered the price even more. Finally, when the vendor reached the price that Billie wanted to pay, she returned and purchased the item. Billie put on this performance repeatedly as they moved around Marché de Fer. It was obviously well worth the effort, though, because they exited the market laden with goods purchased at rock-bottom prices.

"Billie, you really should have been an actress," Joyce said jokingly. "Only a videotape could tell the story."

Tired, but delighted, they returned home to spend a quiet evening together.

"Crash! Bang!" A deafening blast forced Mandy bolt upright in bed the next morning. She glanced at her watch. It was only five o'clock and dawn had not yet broken.

"That must have been thunder," she said to herself. "Oh, why did it have to rain today? I was looking forward to our trip to Cap Haitien."

Resigning herself to a rainy morning, she dozed again.

She heard the noise a second time. "That can't be thunder," she decided. "What in the world is going on?"

Springing up, she raced into the living room, colliding directly with Joyce.

"Aunt Joyce, what's happening?" she asked, anxiously.

"I really don't know, but it's an awful commotion," Joyce said. "Something strange is afoot."

They moved to the window and peered through the curtains in the dimness of the early dawn. Quickly they retreated with rising panic at what they saw on the street below. They rushed into Billie's room and found her sleeping, totally oblivious to what was going on.

"Billie!" cried Joyce, shaking her awake. "Something awful is happening outside. It seems like some sort of military operation."

Billie came fully awake and looked out of the window. Truckloads of uniformed soldiers were moving around the square. The area was flooded with people—some walking, some running. The plaza was cordoned off with thick bands of rope. Policemen were taking up their positions.

Suddenly, a siren wailed and a motorcycle brigade arrived on the scene.

Billie hurried next door to her neighbor to see if he knew what was going on.

Returning, she exclaimed, "Oh my goodness! This is a grand occasion. The President is coming!"

Upon hearing that news, they all breathed a collective sigh of relief.

Her neighbor had asked her excitedly, "Haven't you heard? Today begins the feast of St. Peter. Government officials will be attending a solemn mass at the church before the festival begins."

Donning their housecoats, the threesome moved onto the terrace for a ringside view of the proceedings.

"I didn't hear a word about this," said Billie, completely amazed. "But you couldn't have chosen a better weekend to visit than this one. I've never seen this before in Pétion-ville."

As the sun rose higher that late June morning, they noticed that the square had been transformed totally over-night. Buntings and banners were flying overhead. There was a decidedly festive air among the people who had converged on the area for the occasion.

Just as they settled down to watch, there came a sharp knock at the door.

"Who could that be so early, I wonder?" asked Billie, slightly annoyed.

She peeped through the keyhole and fell silent at what she saw.

"What's wrong?" questioned Joyce.

They heard the knocking again.

"Please open!" a voice commanded. "We will explain," she translated for them.

When Billie unbolted the door, into the apartment marched two starchly-uniformed soldiers, their rifles in full view!

Mandy's heart pounded. Joyce trembled.

The soldiers saluted and then apologized for their sudden arrival. They explained rapidly in French to Billie that they needed to be on duty on her balcony during the morning's activities.

Billie, completely taken aback, pointed speechlessly to the open terrace door.

Politely and unobtrusively, the soldiers took up their positions. The women soon relaxed, returning to their balcony seats to observe the activities.

The sirens mourned again. Several jet-black, sleek and shining limousines halted directly outside of the church. Immaculately dressed, highly-placed officials spilled out. Shortly afterward, the President's entourage arrived. A hush fell over the crowd, momentarily. But they burst into wild cheering as he ceremoniously walked to the church's entrance.

A regally-attired monsignor appeared at the doorway of the church, greeting him. The President bowed low before him and worshipfully followed him into the sanctuary.

Presently, the huge bells in the looming tower overhead signaled to all that the mass had ended. The Presidential party exited and crossed over to the square. The applause of the crowd was deafening. The military and security forces struggled to keep things in check. After a brief ceremony, the festival was declared officially open.

As punctiliously as they arrived, the officials departed. The outriders led the executive procession with sirens blaring. The soldiers on the balcony bid their hostesses adieu and disappeared among their comrades below. With swift precision, the military ensemble stamped through their paces, re-boarded their vehicles, and was off.

The atmosphere changed visibly as the crowd dispersed among the stalls of vendors that were there for the occasion.

"This has been unbelievable!" Mandy exclaimed. "It will be a weekend I'll remember for a very long time."

Billie looked at her watch. It was only eight o'clock in the morning. "We can still make it to Cap Haitien if we start now," she advised.

"I'm ready!" replied the ever-adventurous Joyce. "Let's get going!"

The four-hour journey took them through the many farming communities of Haiti's peasant class. Coffee, sugar, and sisal plantations dotted the area. They were greeted by scores of poorly-clad, hard-working laborers who earned a meager existence on the land. They reached their destination via the new highway that passed through rugged mountain terrain.

Cap Haitien, a seaport city on the northern coast of Haiti, richly abounds in history. Mandy learned while there that it was in this part of the island that the battles for freedom were fought and won. The tranquil, charming city with its pastel-colored houses was in sharp contrast to the rushing, tumbling atmosphere of Port-au-Prince. Of greatest interest to Mandy were the ruins of Sans Souci and La Citadelle, about twenty miles south of the city. The travelers stopped for refreshment at a small café before proceeding to the site of the ruins. While there, an elderly gentleman, a self-styled historian, engaged them in conversation. He assisted his son, the owner of the café, in making the patrons feel welcome. Obviously proud of his country, he unfolded to them, with Billie's translation, the story of the ruins. When Mandy later read the official account, she found, to her delight, that their local storyteller had been surprisingly accurate.

"After independence, Henri Christophe made Haiti prosperous," their narrator advised them.

"He provided schools for our people. He built bridges, roads, and castles. The arts flourished and a printing press was started. He was well deserving of his title, 'King Henri I.'"

"How long did he reign?" Mandy inquired.

"About fifteen years. He built Sans Souci, his magnificent palace, during that time and also La Citadelle, a huge fortress, high on the mountain peak."

"What was the palace like?" asked Joyce.

"It had all of the finery that the King could import from Europe. There were tapestries and draperies, fountains and statues, and a grand staircase. A mountain stream flowed under its marble flooring to keep the palace cool," he grandly explained.

"You almost sound as if you lived at that time," Billie suggested to the old man.

"I wish I had," he continued, "Unfortunately, the King became ill and there were also revolts against him. We are told that he shot himself with a silver bullet rather than surrendering to his enemies."

Mandy felt transported back in time as they viewed the ruins of that once-flourishing period. In the tiny village of Milot, she tried to envision the scenes of nearly two centuries past. She was filled with wonder as she thought of Christophe, the son of slaves, who had such dedication and vision to accomplish the enormous work that he did.

"This seems incredible, doesn't it?" Joyce declared as they stood in the midst of Sans Souci's remains.

Sunlight streamed majestically downward through the now roofless chateau. Their official tour guide pointed out what was left of the private quarters of the long-departed royal family and staff. He indicated also where the banquet halls, reception rooms, and courtyard had been.

"The view from the top of La Citadelle is fantastic," advised Billie. "Are you adventurous enough to go up?"

"Why not?" Mandy exclaimed. "Let's go!"

The visitors gazed in awe at the relics of the mountain stronghold. Three thousand feet up high, they reached, at last, the famous Citadelle Lafèrriere. They inspected what was left of the massive stone walls, the barracks, gun galleries, and rusting cannon balls.

"These are lasting reminders of the military might of that era," noted Joyce, grimly.

Hiking onward to the Upper Court, Joyce and Mandy confirmed Billie's description. The phenomenal view of valley and sea below against a backdrop of lush mountain greenery and a cloudless blue sky was absolutely breathtaking.

The visitors overnighted in Cap Haitien, returning to Pétionville early the next day. Billie secured a large carton for them, into which they packed their newly purchased possessions. True to her word, Madame St. Jacques delivered the lovely gown she made for Mandy. The paintings, souvenirs, and other bric-a-brac were safely tucked away.

When Monsieur Moreau returned them to the airport that Monday evening, Mandy declared, "I can't believe we've spent only a weekend here."

"I agree," said Joyce. "It seems as if we left Jamaica weeks ago."

Billie blew them a kiss as they disappeared into the departure lounge. "Have a great time in St. Thomas!" she called. "Come again soon!"

CHAPTER 5

Voyage To The Virgins

It was nearly midnight when the airport taxi stopped in front of Reverend Christian's home. The curtains were closed shut, but a small light could be seen shimmering through. Obviously, the family had retired for the night. Joyce and Mandy tiptoed up the walkway and pressed the bell lightly. The door quickly opened and Reverend Christian, in nightclothes, greeted them warmly.

"Joyce, Amanda, come right in. Welcome to St. Thomas. I thought perhaps your flight from Haiti had been canceled."

"We were delayed about two hours," Joyce explained. "We're sorry to have gotten you out of bed."

Reverend Christian, a tall, imposing man, was no stranger to Mandy. He was a close friend of her father's and visited New York frequently. She was quite familiar with his stirring sermons that he often preached at her church. Joyce was a welcomed guest at his home whenever she stopped in the island.

"You must be starving after your flight," their host declared. "Erla left a snack for you and said to tell you 'welcome.' She had a really exhausting day with the children."

The next morning Mandy felt tiny hands patting her cheeks, and something else was tugging at the bed linen. She opened her eyes to find a pair of round-faced, mischievous-looking toddlers shaking her awake. She later learned that they were the youngest of the Christian clan, three-year-old twin girls, Ava and Avis.

"Hello little darlings," she greeted them.

"Mommy says wake up," Ava commanded.

"It's morning now," Avis agreed.

Mandy rolled out of bed, showered, dressed, and followed them downstairs. The house was alive and buzzing. The family of eight lived modestly in the heart of Charlotte Amalie, the capital of the U.S. Virgin Islands. Mandy was caught up immediately in the love and warmth that she felt in this home.

The twins ushered their guests to seats at the long dining room table where a mammoth breakfast awaited. Erla Christian, their mother, a short, round, and jolly woman, entered from the kitchen.

"So glad to meet you, Amanda," she intoned, in the strong musical accent of the Virgin Islanders. "Joyce, nice to have you again. Please make yourselves at home."

"It's good to be here and meet you all at last," Mandy replied. "Reverend Christian told us a lot about your family."

Richard, 20, and Warren, 18, had summer jobs in town. Lisa, 16, and 9-year-old Marc, completed the family circle.

Mandy ate ravenously the meal of fried johnnycakes, steamed codfish, scrambled eggs, guava juice, and hot chocolate.

Erla, who took pride in her cooking, smiled broadly.

"How was Haiti?" Warren inquired of the visitors.

"It was really exciting," replied Mandy and recounted animatedly some of their experiences.

"Sounds great!" he exclaimed. "I really must visit there someday."

"We had a very hectic weekend," added Joyce. "But the trip was worth every minute of it."

"We hope you'll enjoy your time here as much," Richard injected. "You should pay a visit to St. Croix and St. John, our sister islands, also.

"I think we're going to Tortola, aren't we, Aunt Joyce?" Mandy replied. "Didn't you say it was pretty close to St. Thomas?"

"That's right," she said. "It's in the British Virgin Islands. But we might be able to take a day trip to St. Croix, though."

"What's on your schedule for today?" Erla asked them.

"We thought we'd take it easy today and rest a bit," Joyce advised. "Tomorrow we'd like to spend the day in town."

"That's fine," said Reverend Christian. "We'd like to have you come with us to church tonight, though. We're having revival meetings this week."

"We'd love to go," said Mandy. "Mom and Dad will be pleased to know that we went, too."

Joyce and Mandy reached the church quite early that evening. They were amazed to see how involved the Christian family members were in the service. Each seemed deeply committed, and they all played some part. Lisa, in her smart usher's outfit, capably escorted them to a pew right up front. Richard took his place at the organ, while Warren tuned his guitar. They and others comprised the spirited band that provided the accompanying music.

Mandy gazed around the large edifice. It was not a grand cathedral by any stretch of the imagination. It was sparsely furnished, its paint chipped in places. Its rough wooden pews had no cushions and were rather uncomfortable. No silver chalices or lighted candles adorned its altar. Yet Mandy drew from its quiet simplicity a strength that was hard to describe.

"Isn't that a lovely mural?" Joyce whispered.

Mandy glanced at the wall behind the pulpit. A restful pastoral scene was depicted there of a shepherd leading his flock over a verdant hillside. "It certainly is," she replied. "I'm really glad that we came."

The church quickly filled to overflowing with people. There was an air of expectancy in the congregation. They had come from throughout the island to hear the visiting evangelist. People of all ages were there. Elderly ladies with their perennial straw hats lined the pews. Young people carrying Bibles and hymnbooks, men who had arrived on bicycles, women, and children all came to join in worship.

Suddenly, the drums rolled and the organ grew louder. When the crowd glanced back, Mandy craned her neck also. From the rear of the church, hands clapping and with lively steps, the choir sang and marched toward the platform. The smaller children led the way.

To her surprise, little Avis and Ava were among them, singing lustily and moving in step to the music. "We're marching to Zion, beautiful, beautiful Zion!" she heard as they passed.

She and Joyce exchanged smiles and joined the audience as they clapped. As the choir moved onward, they glimpsed Marc among the older kids in the procession. He waved at them and pointed them out to his singing partner beside him.

As the choir took their places in their loft on the platform, Reverend Christian and Reverend C. A. Walker, the evangelist, made a grand appearance. Dressed in flowing black robes, they strode impressively onto the rostrum from a private entrance.

"Let the church say 'Amen!'" a familiar female voice loudly appealed.

With hands raised and fervor unmatched, the congregation shouted in reply, "Amen! Praise the Lord!"

Mandy glanced forward to see none other than Erla Christian at the microphone! She and Joyce sat dumbfounded as they watched her take command of the gathering like a person transformed.

With mellow voice and arms upraised, she led them, with vitality, in hymns and choruses. Interspersed with the singing, people stood and testified publicly of the goodness of God. As Erla encouraged them, the music swelled to a grand crescendo. The crowd took to its feet, swaying and clapping in perfect rhythm. Several persons danced in the aisles. All were totally engrossed in the worship. Mandy and Joyce were spellbound, and, understandably, breathless by the end of Erla's contribution.

When Reverend Christian came forward to welcome all who came, he was applauded and warmly received by the congregation. He, obviously, was loved and well-respected by the people.

Just as Mandy relaxed in her pew and prepared herself to listen to the sermon, she could hardly believe what she heard.

"Before I present the speaker, ladies and gentlemen, will Misses Amanda Rivers and Joyce Rosewell please stand and greet the audience?"

Mandy was speechless. Her knees trembled as she found her feet and turned to face the vast assembly. Thankfully, Joyce, never lost for words, quickly obliged him and spoke on behalf of them both.

"Good old Aunt Joyce to the rescue," Mandy thought, relieved. She could only manage a weak smile as she sat down.

Introductions over, Reverend Walker, a suave, articulate, gentleman, moved to the lectern.

Before he even uttered a word, however, a woman in the rear of the church shouted, "Preach it, brother!"

A ripple of laughter floated through the crowd as the youthful, eligible bachelor began his message. Thoroughly familiar with his text, he used no written notes to make his points and immediately captivated the crowd. They punctuated his sermon with replies of encouragement as he spurred them on to heights of faith. The young itinerant preacher had so inspired the crowd that, by the end of his message, many surged forward to the altar in penitence and consecration.

Mandy, who had been among them, discussed it later that night. "I was deeply moved by the message," she acknowledged to Reverend Christian.

"You have taken a wonderful step," he assured her. "A living faith is something that each of us needs."

She looked forward to sharing her experience that night with her family back home.

The next day, with Joyce and Lisa as her guides, Mandy wended her way through the busy city of Charlotte Amalie, one of the Caribbean's leading shopping meccas. The jostling crowd reminded her of downtown Nassau or Port-au-Prince. She noticed that some of the streets had strange European-sounding names and remarked on it.

"We once were a colony of Denmark," explained Lisa. "In 1917, the United States government bought our three islands and that made us all American citizens."

"What are St. John and St. Croix like?" Mandy inquired.

"St. Croix is much quieter than St. Thomas. It's the largest of the three islands with the towns of Fredericksted and Christiansted at either end of it. Many of the people living there originally came from Puerto Rico, which is also close by."

"I'm told that St. John is really for honeymooners," Joyce injected, with a twinkle.

Mandy giggled. "I'll save that trip until the next time I come then," she replied.

Lisa took them to a shopping plaza in the heart of the city's commercial district. They first passed along the huge deep water harbor where cruise ships and cargo boats that ply the Caribbean waters were anchored. The vast amount of produce and merchandise that supply the islands' industries was being loaded and offloaded. They were told that this port is the busiest in the region. Dotting the rising hilltops beyond were the villas and mansions of the island's aristocratic families.

Thousands of tourists skittered in and out of the myriad shops in the plaza. They were dressed, typically, in shorts, white socks, and tennis shoes. They were bedecked with cameras and toted bulging shopping bags. The local folk, casually dressed in T-shirts and jeans, contributed also to the rush and madness.

"Today must be your lucky day," declared Lisa as they paused for a quick bite at lunchtime. "Most of the stores are having sales. You're just in time for the bargains."

That's when she noticed the look of dismay on Mandy's face.

"My purse is missing," Mandy anxiously replied.

"Missing?" responded Joyce, distressed. "Did you drop it somewhere?"

"I don't know," said Mandy, now quite distraught. "My wallet, passport, and keys are all gone!"

The trio retraced their steps, searching everywhere for the lost handbag, but to no avail.

"I'm afraid it's been stolen," Lisa said, reluctantly. "I think we should report it to the police."

Mandy felt as if her vacation was totally ruined. A rush of thoughts filled her mind.

"How can I leave here without my passport? Will I be able to get a new one? I have no more money to spend on the trip!"

"There's a police station a few blocks over," Lisa informed.

"Yes," agreed Joyce." "We'd better go there."

Dejectedly, Mandy turned out of the plaza to file her complaint.

Just as they were about to cross the intersection, however, they heard someone calling behind them, "Miss! Miss! Just a minute! Is this yours?"

They turned to find the young store clerk running to catch up with them.

Mandy breathed a sigh of great relief. "Yes, yes, that's mine," she cried, noticing the elusive pocketbook in his hand. "Thank you so much! Where was it?"

"We found it lying on the counter right after you left the store. We've been hunting all around the plaza ever since to see if we could find you."

"That was really kind of you," Joyce commended him. "It's nice to see that people here really care."

"I told you this was your lucky day!" exclaimed Lisa as they resumed their shopping expedition.

The next morning, as they disembarked from the airboat, Mandy exclaimed, "This was quite an experience!"

Erla, the twins, and Mandy had just landed on St. Croix for a day trip.

"See how close we are to St. Thomas?" explained Erla. "It's only forty miles away. I was born here in Christiansted, so this is really my home you know."

"*Now* you can say you've been to the Virgin Islands," chuckled Luther, her brother, who had come to meet them. "Didn't Joyce come with you?"

"She's spending the day with some other friends in St. Thomas," Mandy replied. "She sends you her best regards."

The twins exploded with laughter as their uncle scooped them up in his large, strong arms.

Mandy remarked as she drank in the tranquil serenity of this tropical paradise, "This island is very different from St. Thomas. Where has all the rushing gone?"

Luther laughed. "St. Thomians think we move too slowly over here. But sooner or later, like Erla here, they come to get away from it all."

"We're here! We're here!" sang Avis and Ava in unison as their uncle drove up the shady, palm-fringed driveway of his home.

Luther was an architect as well as a small farmer. His house was one of the many Great Houses that was built years ago by the former Danish planters. Although several lay in ruins around the island, his was beautifully restored to its former gracefulness. He and his wife, Lorna, a talented interior decorator, painstakingly revived its distinctive features.

When they pulled to a stop, the twins burst forth, bombarding the house like miniature tornadoes.

"This is positively gorgeous!" exclaimed Mandy as she gazed around the grounds.

The surrounding gardens were a symphony of flowers. Artfully-shaped casuarina trees formed a border with the acres of vegetables growing beyond.

"Let's go inside first," Luther invited.

Erla beamed proudly as Mandy was shown through the Victorian-style mansion. Its rectangular-shaped steps led up to a louvered gallery. Its stout walls were of cut stone and its sashed windows were overlaid with brick. A skillful blend of antique and modern furniture made the splendid residence breathe a quiet charm. An imported Persian rug covered the cool tiled floor of the main sitting room. Danish pewter, porcelain vases, and crystal chandeliers added to the rich elegance of its interior.

Mandy stared at the huge dining hall into which they had entered. A highly polished mahogany table was the center of attraction.

Soon, Lorna, a smartly dressed and youthful-looking woman, appeared with the squealing twins in tow. "Hi there!" she greeted. "Nice to have you with us."

Erla hugged her warmly and gave her news of the family.

The couple later took their guests on a jaunt through the historic area of downtown Christiansted. In addition to viewing the Old Danish Post Office and Customs House on the waterfront, they visited old Fort Christiansvaern and the stately 200-year-old Governor's Palace.

The remainder of the day was spent relaxing on one of St. Croix's dazzling beaches. They savored the delightful picnic lunch that Lorna had packed for them on the peaceful, uncluttered, seashore. The cool, steady breezes of the trade winds cooled the heat of the midday sun. Spreading out before them like a giant indigo and turquoise blanket, the sea rose and fell in a gentle cadence.

Released from their usual city confines, Ava and Avis built sandcastles and combed the shores like captives set free.

"Tomorrow we leave for the British Virgin Islands," Mandy informed her hosts.

"You'll enjoy it over there," Luther assured her. "Be sure to visit the 'Baths' on Virgin Gorda."

"I believe it's on our schedule," she replied.

"It must be fascinating for you to be visiting the various islands," declared Lorna.

Mandy mused for a moment, and then responded, "It certainly is, and each place we've visited has been so different from the last one."

"What's on the rest of your itinerary?" inquired Erla.

"After Tortola, we'll head for Antigua, then Dominica. That will take us to the halfway point of our journey. We'll spend a longer time in Barbados where Joyce lives, then on to the Grenadines, Trinidad, and, finally, Curaçao."

On her return to St. Thomas that evening, Mandy related to her aunt, "I enjoyed every minute of our time in St. Croix."

"It's so restful over there," Joyce agreed, "and Lorna and Luther really make you feel welcome."

Lisa wandered in to help them pack before their early morning flight to Tortola.

"Even though your time here was so short, we're sure going to miss you," she told them.

"Wouldn't it be great if you could visit me next summer in New York?" asked Mandy. "I'd love to have you."

"There's nothing I'd like better. I'll see if I can get Daddy to agree."

Mandy saw the British Flag, called the Union Jack, flying as the tiny airplane landed after the fifteen-minute flight. She knew that Tortola is the largest of forty pint-sized islands that comprise the British Virgin Islands.

"I've never been here before, but I've heard that this is a sailor's paradise," Joyce remarked as they drove the short distance along the coastline to Road Town, the capital.

Schooners, sloops, and yachts of all descriptions were berthed in the sundrenched marinas. Flags of many countries flew from their overhead masts.

"I read that the lobster and seafood here are really special," said Mandy.

"You're right, Miss. Do enjoy them," their taxi driver interjected.

"This is really cozy," Mandy exclaimed when later they were settled in the quaint little guesthouse.

The sparsely furnished, but immaculately clean, wooden house was divided into small and large bedrooms. Each contained a tiny shower and dressing area.

The owners, Horace and Maude Bristol, lived for years on the island after emigrating there from Britain. Their delicious meals were served family-style, and the guests quickly became acquainted with each other. Mandy observed that the dozen or so guests accommodated there were quite an interesting mix. She learned a lot during her short time there.

"I come here every year," declared the old retired colonel in his thick German brogue. "It's my second home now, and I always stay here with the Bristols."

"How did you learn about Tortola?" Joyce inquired.

"My first visit here was years ago during the Second World War," he explained. "I fell in love with this place and said I'd come back some day and here I am."

"We won a honeymoon prize trip," the young Canadian couple informed. "It was really a lucky break for us."

"We're here for our summer holiday," they learned from the Josephs, a Vincentian family of four. "We visit a different island every year."

"Tell me about St. Vincent," Mandy, always eager for new information, inquired.

"It's quite far from here," Dougal, a teenager, advised. "It's mountainous in sections and there's a volcano, called 'Soufriere' at the top of one of them."

Mandy, surprised, pressed him. "A volcano? Is it active?"

"It last erupted a few years ago," Carlyle, his brother, informed. "Thousands of people had to be evacuated from the area around it."

"We were told that the dust from the crater reached as far away as Barbados, our neighboring island," their mother explained.

"Do you ever worry that it might happen again?" asked Joyce.

"We do," injected their father. Then he added humorously, "But life goes on. We can only hope and pray that it will only gurgle gently instead of blowing its top like it did the last time."

Joyce and Mandy shared some of their island adventures thus far with their new acquaintances.

Later on, niece and aunt went on a walking excursion through the town. They browsed through the shops of the tiny capital's main street. The shopkeepers were extremely polite and helped them make several selections. Mandy was especially pleased with the black coral jewelry on sale and purchased a few pieces as souvenirs.

As they waited that afternoon at the airport, Mandy laughingly asked Joyce, "How would you like to visit 'Dead Man's Chest' or 'Prickly Pear'?"

She was reading to Joyce from the travel brochure the list of names of the other islands and cays that comprise that land of unspoiled beauty.

"No thanks, I'll stick to inhabited places like 'Jost Van Dyke' and 'Peter Island', if you please," Joyce replied, smiling.

The nine-seat mini-aircraft that they awaited took them to Virgin Gorda, a five-minute hop away. On arrival, Wallace Wheatley, a friend of their Tortola hosts, met them. He was a native of Virgin Gorda and served as their local guide while there. On the map the island was a tiny dot in the ocean. Slumbering in tropical greenery, it was, by far, the most naturally beautiful of all the places they had seen so far. A feeling of solitude engulfed them. Here it seemed as if nature was untouched by mankind. Along the windswept shoreline sea grapes grew in wild abandon. Further inland, ferns, mosses, and other vegetation intertwined themselves with varying species of trees.

"Mrs. Bristol mentioned that you're anxious to visit the 'Baths,'" said Wallace.

"We sure are," replied Mandy. "So many people have told us not to miss them. Am I correct that they're a natural rock formation?"

"I guess that's a way of describing them," he affirmed. "They must have been here on our island for thousands of years."

They drove for a while down a craggy, unpaved road toward the ocean.

"We'll have to go the rest of the way on foot," Wallace informed them.

Several other tourists joined them as they continued the downward trek, arriving at last at the eerily beautiful 'Baths.'

An enormous weatherworn stone faced them, as if fiercely guarding the entrance. It had a natural opening at its base.

"Do you remember how to crawl?" Wallace asked them, laughing.

They each got down on all fours, scrambling through to the other side.

"This is simply awesome!" Mandy exclaimed as she gazed around at this unusual natural wonder.

They had entered an area of caves that were formed by huge boulders piled one on top of the other. It felt as if they were inside of a grand cathedral. The ocean flowed in among the boulders, forming shallow shimmering pools around them.

Some visitors, clad in bathing suits, swam between the rocks to the sea beyond. Joyce waded, knee deep, enjoying the refreshing salty sprays. Mandy emptied the entire roll of film in her camera, wanting to capture this utterly amazing sight for the folks back home.

Back at the Bristols that evening, Joyce informed the guests, "We're off to Antigua tomorrow. As we continue our journey southward, we want to include the excitement of the Leeward Islands also."

"Good luck! Bon chance!" Carlyle and Dougal wished them. "You should write about your travels some day."

CHAPTER 6

Leeward Landmarks

Early next morning they winged their way south to the island of Antigua. The small regional aircraft that brought them flew low over the cluster of neighboring islands. It was a clear day, and the captain pointed out to the passengers, St. Kitts, Nevis, and Montserrat. Joyce, who had visited the Leewards many times before, gave Mandy an impromptu history lesson about these tiny isles.

"St. Kitts is really a nickname for St. Christopher. It was the first British colony in the Eastern Caribbean. St. Kitts and Nevis together make up one independent nation."

"Do a lot of tourists go there?" asked Mandy.

"More and more they do," Joyce explained. "But the charming beauty of these twin islands and their tranquil lifestyle have made them secret playgrounds of the wealthy for years."

"Tell me about Montserrat, though," Mandy urged. "I understand that only a few years ago it all but disappeared."

"You're right," confirmed Joyce. "A slumbering, gurgling volcano, high atop a mountain on this island, literally blew its top. Unbelievably, the entire island had to be evacuated. Only a few stalwart people remain still living there."

"What was life like before the volcano?" asked Mandy, "And where did all of the people go?"

"Montserrat was once known as the 'Emerald Isle.' Irish settlers populated it a few centuries ago before the French and English arrived. Until recently, you could still hear traces of the Irish brogue in the accents of the people. They were peaceful and comfortable in their beautiful island home. When the volcano blew, the people that left the island dispersed far and wide. Some went to England, Canada, and the United States. Fortunately, however, because the neighboring islands are so close, many relocated there to join family and friends."

Mandy learned that the sand on Montserrat's beaches is black because of its volcanic origins.

As the airplane approached Antigua, Mandy noticed that, unlike the other three islands, it was flat and dry with a few rolling hills. Remnants of sugar mills from the old plantation days were evident as they drove from Coolidge Airfield. From their hilltop hotel, they were afforded a marvelous view of St. John's, the capital, and its beautiful harbor.

"We timed it perfectly," declared Mandy as they traversed through St. John's later that sweltering July afternoon. "I've always wanted to experience a West Indian carnival. I knew it was too late in the year for us to get in on Trinidad's."

"That's right," Joyce replied. "Trinidad 'does their thing' around mid-February just before the Lenten season. They call it 'The Greatest Show on Earth.'"

"I hear that Antigua's carnival is quite a celebration, though," Mandy exclaimed. "I'm so glad we're in time to see it."

The streets were ablaze with color, and the festive spirit was everywhere. The weeklong show was about to begin. Mandy learned that three main ingredients bring Caribbean carnivals to life: the magnificent steel band orchestras, the spectacular costumes, and calypso—the catchy, rhythmic indigenous music. They were shortly to observe how carnival would transform this normally casual, restful island into a leaping, jumping, bouncing beehive of activity.

That day, the streets of the city, usually only moderately filled with shoppers, were bursting at the seams. Busy store clerks were rushing to accommodate the many visitors who had arrived for carnival. Mandy bought a few items, including a hand-woven straw bag. Joyce selected a lovely locally-made Sea Island cotton blouse.

"Sea Island cotton is one of Antigua's largest agricultural exports," a saleslady explained.

As they walked around the town, it was interesting to note the baroque style architecture from the colonial days among the buildings and monuments they passed.

Returning to their hotel, they stopped first at a colorful wayside market to purchase some pineapples. "Our pineapples are the sweetest in all of the West Indies," the aproned vendor proudly declared.

Mandy discovered when she sampled them that the vendor had been absolutely correct. The succulent fruit, cultivated widely on the island for centuries, was the best she'd ever tasted. She ordered it daily for breakfast after that.

Three flight attendants, named Hyacinth, O'Neall, and Olive, came by the next morning to take Joyce and Mandy on an island tour. They lived in Antigua and were long-time friends of Joyce's. Their first stop was English Harbor, a famous historical site located some fifteen miles away from St. John's on the other side of the island. It was once England's major naval base in the Caribbean.

Olive explained, "It was from this beautiful natural harbor that the eminent Lord Nelson of Britain sailed when he fought his many eighteenth century sea battles in the area."

Hyacinth winked at Joyce and said, "Doesn't Lord Nelson's statue stand in all of its glory in the center of Bridgetown, Barbados, your adopted home?"

They stopped for a while at Nelson's Dockyard where, long ago, the Royal Navy established facilities to refurbish its ships. It was named after the famous Admiral who had his base of operations there. Mandy was able to view the old buildings, now restored, which were of great importance during that era.

"This whole complex has become a top tourist attraction ' and yachting center," O'Neall explained.

Mandy, indeed, noticed the many yachts with their tall-masted sails, which were anchored offshore. It reminded her very much of those she'd seen in Tortola. She learned that over the past three to four decades, English Harbor had become a yachting magnet in the West Indies.

"Perhaps you're wondering who the people are aboard those gorgeous sloops," O'Neall volunteered.

"Are they mainly Europeans?" asked Mandy. "They all seem to have glorious suntans."

"They hail from all over the world," he explained. "Some are private owners of the vessels who have come here to have their boats serviced. But many have chartered them for carefree floating vacations on the high seas."

"This area of the island has really benefited from the yachting operations," Olive continued. "In addition to the restaurants and other businesses that have opened, many of our local people have found jobs repairing and refitting the ships."

"The end of April each year is Sailing Week here," Hyacinth advised them. "The Regatta is quite a big event, with local skippers competing against internationally-known captains in the races."

"Sounds like lots of fun," Joyce remarked. "I'm sure the spectators enjoy it as much as the sailors."

After a leisurely lunch, they chatted awhile with some seafaring visitors and then moved on for a swim at Dickerson Bay, one of Antigua's sparkling beaches.

"I'd like to have a look at my costume," said Hyacinth, as they later made their way back to St. John's.

"Let's stop and see it," agreed Olive. "This will be an interesting experience for Mandy."

Hyacinth was referring to her participation in one of the carnival bands. For the third consecutive year, she was in the same band, a fairly large one, with over one hundred members. Each year the band selected a subject to depict that sparks the imagination. This year its choice was "Kingdom of the Insects." Bedecked in their magnificent costumes, band members would participate in the grand "road march" accompanied by a wonderful steel band.

"Trinidadians call it 'playing mas,'" Hyacinth explained. "It's one big masquerade party, complete with marching, dancing, and parading!"

"It will dizzy your senses when you see the massive street 'jump up' and the colorful bands moving through," injected O'Neall.

"Yes," laughed Olive. "'Playing mas' also refers to the wild abandon that seems to overtake visitors and locals alike when the carnival is in full swing."

O'Neall turned onto a road on the outskirts of the city and stopped in front of a building that seemed to be some type of community center. It was buzzing with activity.

Mandy stared incredulously at what she saw. It was obvious that every ounce of talent and imagination was being put into creating the wonderful carnival costumes. Several band members were trying them on as finishing touches were applied. They were hoping that they would capture the prize this year for the best-costumed band. Their costumes consisted of a panorama of creatures from the insect world. Some of them would be on foot while others would ride gracefully atop colorful floats. A section of the band would comprise a group of butterflies. Mandy watched as their huge multicolored wings were being completed. They were created from cloth, wire, rings, and an odd assortment of other materials, such as paper, wood, pipe cleaners, beads, yarn, clothes pins, cardboard, styrofoam, and artificial flowers.

Hyacinth would be in the beetle section. Grasshoppers and spiders would be depicted also. The Queen Bee would sit on a royal float, while her loyal subjects buzzed around her.

"I can't wait to see the band in action when the parade begins!" Mandy exclaimed.

That night at dinner a waitress animatedly informed them, "The countdown has started for the reigning calypso monarch."

Mandy learned that each year there's a grand competition to select the top calypso tune of the carnival. The singers, called calypsonians, vie with each other for the crown.

They are affectionately dubbed nicknames such as "Lord Prosperous," "The Mighty Tiger," and "King Dinosaur," among others.

O'Neall returned that night to take them to the finals. A huge crowd had gathered to cheer on their favorite competitors.

"Try to catch the words if you can," O'Neall advised. "Some of the lyrics are comical and describe the strange behavior of people. Others are quite serious, however, with commentary on important current events."

Mandy tried to follow the rapid staccato intonations of the singers as they burst into song on stage. She finally gave up, though. The crowd roared with laughter at the wit and antics of the singers as the accompanying music spurred them on. It was fun to watch it all anyway.

It was way past midnight when the judges finally made their decision and Carnival King was crowned. The Mighty Tiger, for the fourth straight year, won again by a landslide.

Joyce and Mandy wearily climbed into bed that night looking forward to the next day's events.

The following morning Mandy and Joyce arrived early to take up good positions. The cultural extravaganza was indeed a massive theater in the streets. Their friends certainly had not exaggerated when they described the road march. The steel band orchestras were already in full gear. They were composed of talented young people playing spirited tunes on discarded and recycled oil drums. The players, dressed in colorful uniformed shirts and blouses, used their drumsticks in perfect rhythm, as the sound of steel filled the air.

Soon, the first band arrived, its rollicking, frolicking members depicting a magical war scene from Ancient Egypt. The headgear of the soldiers was fantastic, as were their swords, shields, and spears. Their golden boots shimmered in the morning sunshine as their leaders urged them along.

On and on the bands marched in endless numbers as the sun rose higher in the sky. Vendors selling food, drinks, and delicacies of all descriptions kept the crowds well supplied.

"Here they come, Aunt Joyce," Mandy gleefully cried as the Insect Kingdom came into view.

They both gazed open-mouthed at the captivating spectacle. The band suddenly transported the onlookers to a huge and fanciful forest. There, among the foliage and wild flowers, the glorious insects reigned.

"Have you spotted Hyacinth yet?" asked Joyce.

"Yes, and she and the beetles are hard at work in the woodlands," replied Mandy, laughing.

The band members accepted the thunderous applause of the crowd as they continued on their way.

"I think they might win," Mandy said.

"I'd hate to be one of the judges," Joyce replied. "It would just be too hard for me to decide. The colors, the fantasy, the exuberance, and the inventiveness of all of the bands are just incredible."

They were very happy when Hyacinth's band made first place runner-up in the contest.

At the end of their long week of reveling, Mandy and Joyce left Antigua. While waiting at the airport to depart on a hot afternoon, a middle-aged Swedish visitor engaged them in conversation.

"We're headed for the Windward Islands," Mandy told him.

"My wife and I are in-transit for a flight to Trinidad," he offered. "I'll be working there for a year on contract with an engineering firm."

"I'm sure you'll find island living very different," Mandy suggested, trying hard not to stare at his woolen tweed suit.

"I'm sure I will. I've traveled throughout Europe, but never before to this part of the world," he said.

While they spoke, a tall, blonde, fortyish woman approached. Her attire seemed even more out of sync than his. She wore a long-sleeved white dress with a gold belt at her waist. With heavy makeup and perfectly manicured nails, she sported a broad felt hat, more befitting a vacation in the Swiss Alps.

"This must be your wife," Mandy acknowledged, as he nodded in the affirmative. The women courteously exchanged pleasantries.

When they'd moved on, Joyce jested, "I wonder who advised them about the weather down here? You certainly can see some oddities at times."

Mandy chuckled and said, "I can see, Aunt Joyce, that traveling is really a passing parade."

CHAPTER 7

Winding Windwards

It seemed as if the forty-seat inter-island carrier would miss the runway. The tiny airstrip was dwarfed by the myriad groves of coconut trees that surrounded it. The pilot, however, was obviously a seasoned navigator and seemed intimately familiar with his route. He touched down smoothly on the tarmac. The passengers cheered and thanked him as they deplaned in the island of Dominica.

The day was warm and humid and a heavy mist hung low overhead. It was typical weather for the season in this land of many rivers and mountains.

Mandy's attention was attracted to the boisterous din of the taxi drivers.

"Right here, Miss."

"This way, sir!"

"Your first time in Dominica?"

Each of them jostled to ferry the travelers to Roseau, the capital, where, no doubt, all of them were going.

The long, tiresome journey over twisting, tortuous, rough roads, with their steep gradients and hairpin bends, was like nothing Mandy had ever experienced before. This largely rural, nature-endowed island contrasted sharply with the urban centers they'd left behind. Tiny houses dotted hillsides in remote, unkempt villages. Children played while women washed clothes on the many riverbanks. The ninety-minute trip was exhausting yet exhilarating as the road wound endlessly over craggy mountain precipices high above the sparkling blue sea.

"Whew, that was close!" the passengers exclaimed repeatedly, as the taxi came dangerously close to the road's edges. Most had no protective guardrails in case there was an accident.

Joyce and Mandy wondered if they would make it safely to Roseau. Although packed in like sardines and decidedly uncomfortable, they still enjoyed the marvelous scenery. They passed through rugged forested areas and verdant flora in lush sun-kissed gorges and grassy knolls.

"I can see why this island is nicknamed 'a botanist's paradise,'" Joyce remarked. "How totally different it is from the other islands we've seen!"

"Yes," Mandy murmured. "I have the feeling that there's something very unusual about this island, but I can't quite put my finger on what it is."

The driver explained that they had come to the largest of the windward group of islands in the Eastern Caribbean. "We have three-hundred-sixty-five rivers—one for every day of the year," he proudly affirmed, "and, we are the most mountainous by far."

Suddenly, two heavily-laden banana trucks bore down the road sharply approaching them. They were carrying their precious cargo, the island's main crop, to the banana boxing plants for shipment abroad. Their driver interrupted his explanations to banter with the truck drivers. They harangued each other good naturedly in Patois, the local dialect.

"It sounds something like Creole that we heard back in Haiti," Mandy suggested to her aunt.

The driver, overhearing her, proceeded to explain.

"We are sandwiched between two French islands—Martinique and Guadeloupe. France once owned our island also and our Patois is broken French. There is a lot of travel among our three territories."

Mandy's thoughts drifted as the journey wore on. They ascended to a flatter area that was signposted "Pont Casse." Suddenly, the taxi swerved. It careened left, then right, then left again, jolting the terrified passengers repeatedly. It seemed as if the driver had lost control of the taxi.

"What's wrong? Do you have a flat tire?"

"Hit your brakes!" they cried.

"I've missed it!" the driver shouted disgustedly and swore loudly.

The passengers exchanged mystified glances as the car took an even course again.

A Caribbean child. The expressive eyes and innocent
face are typical of children of the West Indies.
Photo by Leonard Higginson, New York, N.Y.

"What did you miss?" Joyce plucked up the courage to ask.

"The agouti!" he cried. "Didn't you see it run across our path?"

A seasoned visitor to the island was among them in the taxi. He relieved their bewilderment and explained, "An agouti is a small wild boar that roams free in the forestlands here. Its meat is considered quite a delicacy to some of the local inhabitants."

Mandy and the others could scarcely believe what they had heard. Their chauffeur had deliberately tried to hit the animal despite carrying a full carload of passengers! "We could have been killed," she thought, shuddering at the thought.

Much later, the driver advised them that they were, at last, near Roseau. At that point, they were between the two small villages of Mahaut and Massacre. They passed a large factory where the sweet smell of coconut oil pervaded them.

"Our soaps and cosmetics are manufactured here," they were informed. "We ship it out to several countries."

The travelers were greatly relieved when they crossed a narrow bridge at one end of the town. The Roseau River flowed beneath it. Pedestrians, vendors, and all types of vehicles jostled and thronged across it. Mandy prayed that it would bear the weight of this heavy traffic congestion.

As they approached the center of the quaint, busy town, a curious sight arrested them. The traffic came to a halt, giving way to a strange procession. An extensive row of mournful people, dressed in purple, black, and white, were clutching wreaths and flowers. They slowly walked behind an open van bearing a wooden coffin. The cortege had exited from a church nearby and was moving toward a cemetery. A quiet hush engulfed the area until the funeral passed.

"This trip certainly has been educational," acknowledged Mandy to Joyce. "I'm learning a lot about the various customs of people in other lands."

Later at their hotel, Joyce yawned and said, "That trek over the mountains was more like a safari. I'm totally beat."

Mandy laughed. "Why don't you take a nap?" she replied. "I think I'll move around the hotel before dinner. I spied a gift shop and a swimming pool when we checked in."

"Speaking of safaris," Mandy ventured to her aunt as they breakfasted early next morning, "the hotel manager told me that tours to places of interest on the island are available."

"What do you have in mind?"

"I'd like to visit the Carib Indian reservation and also the Trafalgar Falls. I hear they are spectacular."

"That sounds like a lot for one day. But I think I've recovered from yesterday's journey from the airport," Joyce replied with renewed vitality. "Besides, I didn't get to see either of those places the last time I was here."

The hotel provided boxed lunches for them and made arrangements for their excursion with Dorian Seraphine, a popular Land Rover driver. His high, Jeep-like vehicle was fit for the rugged terrain.

Dorian, jokingly, told them, "Don't show up with frilly sundresses or sandals, please. Be prepared to rough it."

So, clad in slacks, shirts, sweaters, and tennis shoes Mandy and Joyce were soon on their way.

The tiny hamlet of Trafalgar was about half an hour's ride away. They discovered that it was the headquarters for the country's major hydroelectric power station. Electricity was supplied to areas several miles away. From this important point, the source of the power was the lovely Trafalgar Falls. Dorian suggested that they view the Falls first and then visit the power plant.

The Falls were quite a scenic wonder. Mandy learned that its glistening, rushing waters originated from three different rivers. When they converged, they formed the Falls, which plummeted over a precipice to a valley below.

"I wish I could stay here all day," Mandy remarked. "It's really a beautiful sight."

"Yes, but we'd better move on to the power plant though," Joyce advised. "Remember that Dorian said it's quite a long journey to the Carib reservation."

They found the electrical center at the end of the village. It was a maze of machines, equipment, and operations. A plant official showed them around, explaining in simple terms the functions of the enormous generators.

"This is my first time in a power station," Mandy explained.

"It's the first time for most of our visitors," their guide assured her. "But we welcome all who come."

When they returned to the Land Rover, Dorian informed, "We'll head east now on the Imperial road. It's the quickest way to get where we're going."

Passing through the island's interior, they saw endless acres of produce under cultivation on the many large estates. Grapefruit, oranges, bananas, and limes were all pointed out.

"How long is your stay in our island?" Dorian inquired.

"We're scheduled to leave on Friday for Barbados," Joyce responded. "This is the ninth island that we've visited since we started."

"That's quite a grand tour!" he exclaimed. "Before you leave Dominica, though, you should really take a trip to Scott's Head at the southern tip of the island."

"Is there something special there?" Joyce queried.

"It's another of our tourist attractions. On a clear day you can view the island of Martinique, our neighbor. But most interesting about it is the natural land border that divides the Atlantic Ocean from the Caribbean Sea."

"Tell us more about that," Mandy urged him.

"You can actually feel and taste the difference between the two great waters," he explained. "If you go to the Atlantic side first, you'll find a rough, pounding surf with furious waves and breakers. It's like that all along the windward, or eastern side of the island, where swimming is really not advised."

"So is the Caribbean side just the opposite?" Joyce inquired.

"Exactly. The water on the leeward side is less salty and is calmer and much more ideal for swimming. You can walk easily from one side to the other, and the area is great for picnicking."

"If we go there, it will have to be on Thursday," suggested Mandy.

"Yes. We have some friends in Roseau to visit tomorrow," Joyce agreed. "They'll never forgive us if we leave without seeing them, and they already know that we're here."

By mid-afternoon they reached the village of Salybia where the Carib Reserve was located. Mandy learned that Dominica is the only island in the Caribbean that maintains a special area for its original inhabitants, the Caribs.

Dorian introduced them to the Carib chief, who he knew from this leader's many visits to Roseau. In turn, he appointed a sociable youngster to show them around the settlement.

"We've lived on this site for over seventy-five years," the young man explained. "We grow our own crops and do river fishing for a livelihood. Many of our women weave baskets."

Dorian had explained on the way there that the Caribs had once been very warlike. Over the years, however, they took on a more peaceful lifestyle. Although their numbers have dwindled to only a few hundred people, they still maintain a rather isolated existence.

As they passed some local craftsmen, their guide informed them, "These elderly men have been building canoes for many years."

Their weatherworn faces had oriental features, typical of their tribe.

"Do you speak your own language?" Mandy inquired.

"Our language has pretty much died out. Only the older people remember a few words. We speak English and Patois at home."

The visitors browsed through the shops there where many of the locally-made baskets were on sale. Their characteristic brown and beige colors had intricate designs. Mandy and Joyce bought a few for the folks back home.

It was nighttime by the time they returned to Roseau. They were surprised to discover that a group of teachers had checked into their hotel while they were gone. They had come from several islands for an annual convention. Joyce recognized two of them, named Enid and Waldo, from Barbados. She and Mandy joined them for supper.

The hotel chef had prepared some local dishes for the guests' enjoyment. The waitresses in the dining room that evening were neatly attired in outfits similar to their old national costume. Their peasant blouses were scooped-necked with puffed sleeves over colorful three-quarter-length hooped skirts. They wore red plaid bandanas on their heads that were folded cleverly into upraised corners.

Matching scalloped aprons completed their charming apparel.

"Have you ever eaten our mountain chicken?" their waitress eagerly inquired.

"Is that your famous 'crapaud'?" Joyce countered with a twinkle.

"Yes, that's its name in Patois," she replied. "It's really delicious."

"What's mountain chicken?" Enid asked.

"It's frog meat," Joyce explained, "One of Dominica's specialties."

"We also have calaloo tonight, if you prefer," the waitress continued. "It's a stew that contains beef and chicken, local vegetables, and provisions, such as dasheen, tania, and pumpkin. We use a variety of seasonings in it also to make it spicy."

"I'll take a chance on the mountain chicken," Mandy said. "Who will join me?"

"I'll try it, too," said Joyce, while the others settled for the calaloo.

"Have you heard about the hurricane in the area?" Waldo asked as they ate their meal.

"Yes, but I hope it will drift away like the first one did earlier this season," Enid exclaimed.

Mandy learned that the hurricane season extends from May to October each year in the Caribbean. Each of the islands at some time in its history has been severely stricken.

"The last big one in Barbados was as long ago as 1955," Waldo informed. "Every year we still take precautions, though."

Mandy, a bit concerned, pressed them. "Does this one sound serious, Waldo?"

"When we were leaving Barbados, the weather report said that it was still a good way off but moving slowly in this direction."

"Don't worry," Enid reassured her, "Hurricanes are very unpredictable. They frequently turn around and blow right out to sea. Besides, the mountains here should serve as great barriers if it should come this way."

Although more relieved, Mandy still prayed that night that the storm would stay out at sea.

The next morning, however, the weather report was rather foreboding:

"The islands of the Eastern Caribbean have been placed on a hurricane watch. Rain is expected to be heavy today, and thunder and lightning are likely. People are advised to remain indoors, if possible. Fishing boats and other small craft should be securely anchored. Occupants of homes in low-lying areas should go to the nearest churches or schools for shelter."

"Sounds ominous," Waldo declared. "The storm must have intensified during the night."

"We certainly can't begin our conference today," Enid stated, regretfully.

A ripple of anxiety floated through the dining room.

"I hope this is only a summer squall," someone said.

Another remarked, "I've always heard that Dominica normally has a higher rainfall than the other islands."

Joyce went to the hotel's front desk. "Where on these grounds is the safest place to take shelter if we need to?" she inquired of the manager.

"I don't think this is really the hurricane," he joked. "Anyway, either your rooms or the sitting room to the left should be quite safe."

Mandy, who took the report very seriously, spoke up and said to the group, "I think we should all stay together."

About an hour later, an eerie stillness gripped the air. Suddenly, a huge gust of wind blew, shaking the window panes in the area in which they'd gathered. Looking out-side, they saw a sheet of galvanized metal sailing through the air. The rain drizzled and then fell in torrents.

The sea nearby began to roar. A few seconds later, they heard a thunderous crash. A tree had become uprooted and toppled over onto the ground. The frightened guests, about thirty-five strong, scampered toward the sitting room to wait out the storm. Lightning laced the sky followed by deafening claps of thunder. The noise of the wind was awe-some as it swooshed, sputtered, bellowed, and wailed.

"This is it!" exclaimed Waldo. "There's no doubt about it. The hurricane's here!"

Some of them wept, while others prayed.

Mandy nearly lost her courage as a lump welled up inside her throat. "Aunt Joyce, I'm really scared. Don't leave me," she pleaded, clutching Joyce's hand.

Joyce, very much in control as usual, comforted her.

The doors of the sitting room were locked but shook as the tempest continued to pound.

"Let's slide some chairs against them," Enid cried. "It's our only hope!"

Desperately, they shoved the furniture over, forming a strong, protective barrier. Fortunately, the room's walls were made of stone and its concrete roof kept them safe.

Sometime later, the din subsided and the trembling band thought it was finally over.

"This may be only the eye of the storm," conjectured the hotel's chef, who, along with other staff members, also took refuge in the sitting room. "We'd better wait in here a while longer."

"I agree," said a teacher from St. Lucia. "We had a hurricane recently and I learned a lot about them. When the eye passes over, the air becomes calm. But then it begins all over again."

The others groaned loudly, but soon discovered that it was best to heed his advice. For, as suddenly as it stopped, the tempest's fury started again. This time it sounded as if a great army was tramping through the town. It continued like this for quite some time, as a feeling of helplessness and hopelessness pervaded the group. They could tell that the gusting gales were wreaking havoc all around outside.

Three hours later, the tumult finally abated and the rain trickled down in a fine sprinkle.

"Has it finally stopped?" implored Mandy.

"It seems as if it's over," the manager declared cautiously. "I'd advise you all to remain where you are for a while longer, though, and don't go outside yet."

He and his staff went out on the grounds to survey the extent of the damage. The shaken guests could hardly move anyway.

A housekeeper reappeared in a flash, trembling.

"You won't believe what I just saw," she chattered. She was completely overcome with emotion. "The entire hotel is in shambles!"

The manager confirmed what she said and told them that the storm was indeed over. The group, warily, moved out of the room. The sight that they saw was indescribable. Chairs and tables were overturned. Broken glass and all kinds of objects were scattered everywhere. The roofing was ripped off in sections, and the swimming pool was full of debris.

A gloomy report captured their attention as a guest turned on a transistor radio.

The announcer from a neighboring island provided this newsflash:

"We've lost all contact with Dominica. But it's definite that the hurricane has battered the island. A British naval vessel in the area that was tracking its path has confirmed this. The extent of injury or damage is still unknown, and governments of the region have expressed much concern. Stand by for further reports."

"Let's check out our room, Mandy," Joyce suggested.

They could hardly open the door as they tread ankle-deep in water. Pushing it open, they were aghast at what they saw. The room bore no resemblance to what it looked like before.

All of their belongings were strewn around the room. Shattered glass was everywhere, and their bed linens were drenched with water from the rain.

"Thank God we left this suitcase locked in the closet," Mandy exclaimed, glad that their precious souvenirs had not been destroyed.

"We certainly can't sleep in here tonight," Joyce muttered. "I wonder how the others fared?"

They made their way down the corridor to Enid's room. She stood there, wordlessly, shaking her head. Mandy peered inside.

"It's just the same as ours," she confirmed.

"It looks as if this will be our living quarters for a while," remarked Waldo, as they returned to the sitting room to ponder their plight.

Mandy observed how closely knit the group of them had become—a camaraderie formed by their common situation.

The manager appeared and provided some depressing information. "All of the electrical power on the island is out, folks. By nightfall we'll be in total darkness. Water pipes are also broken, so we have no running water. Things are in a very bad way," he solemnly advised.

Feelings of panic began to rise among them as they realized the implications of what he just said.

"How long is it likely to be like this?" Joyce inquired.

"It's impossible to say," he replied. "If you think it's awful here at the hotel, you should take a look outside at the town."

"What about food?" asked Mandy. "Is there anything left to eat?"

"That's the good news I have for you. Thank God the kitchen was only slightly damaged. We still have a good supply of cooking gas and a freezer full of food. It should keep us going for a while."

They felt somewhat relieved but wondered how long they would have to stay there on the island.

"I'm going to look around the town," declared Waldo. "I want to see things for myself."

"I'm coming with you," said Joyce, glancing at her watch.

It was nearly two o'clock in the afternoon.

"So am I!" cried Mandy.

Marilyn Noel and Jackie Barker, two other teachers, also went along.

"Be sure to be back before dark," the manager cautioned. "Remember, there will be no lights."

The adventurous band was in no way prepared for what they saw when they ventured out. They gazed, open-mouthed, at the widespread destruction. The fury of the gods had been surely aroused for the town resembled a war zone. Fallen trees and utility poles blocked the roads.

The aftermath of a hurricane. The roof
of a church is totally collapsed.
Photo by Brooks-LaTouche, Barbados, West Indies

Roofless houses, offices, and public buildings stood in naked disarray. Tangled wires and broken objects, flung furiously from their usual places, crammed the gutters of the streets. Grapefruit, oranges, and tree branches littered the alleyways.

"I can't believe this!" Mandy exclaimed. "This isn't possible."

"I'm afraid it is," Waldo replied. "You have to see it to believe it."

They trekked cautiously and silently through the torn and tattered community, gazing at the remnants of a city now gone.

They passed a woman who was crying hysterically as she sat among the remains of her small wooden house. It was now only a heap of boards beside the road. Mandy's heart went out to her, but she felt helpless to assist her. Others sat apathetically. They were stunned by the tragedy that had befallen them. Streets and roads were no longer there, only tangled masses of wood and bricks.

A van filled with moaning people was desperately trying to maneuver its way through the disheveled street where the group was walking.

"Emergency! Emergency! I'm trying to get to the hospital!" called the driver, repeatedly blowing his horn.

The pedestrians then realized that the van was a makeshift ambulance carrying injured people.

"Perhaps we should follow that van," Joyce suggested. "I'm sure the medical staff can use all the help they can get."

"I can't stand the sight of blood," replied Waldo, dubiously. "But maybe I can still lend a hand somehow."

Roofless houses and buildings result from the
havoc wreaked by a hurricane on a tropical island.
Photo by Barbados Govt. Information Service.

It was quite a ways, on foot, to the hospital, and, upon arrival, they met total chaos.

They momentarily forgot their weariness and the incredible sights they had passed on their way there. Literally, hundreds of people had converged there. Many were hurt, hungry, and homeless. Others were there out of curiosity. The group learned that the local prison and the psychiatric hospital both had been destroyed by the hurricane, and, some of the injured inmates and patients sought medical relief or shelter in the main hospital, to which Mandy and the other helpers had come. Nurses, doctors, and volunteer workers were trying, bravely, to sort the true casualties from the onlookers and administer the necessary treatment.

Thankfully, the British ship docked in the harbor, and several of its crew came ashore to help with some of the relief activities. They erected a tarpaulin over an area of the hospital where a portion of its roof had blown off during the storm. This greatly assisted the medical staff in performing their duties, and in sheltering the sick patients.

Immediately, a nurse came hurrying over. "Joyce! There you are," she called. "I was so worried about how you had survived the storm. What a way to spend your vacation!"

"Annette, you look exhausted." Joyce replied. "We were very frightened, of course, during the hurricane. But we're okay now."

She then introduced Mandy, Waldo, and the others. "This is my friend Annette Pierre," she explained. "Mandy and I were going to have dinner with her and her family today."

Turning to Annette, she added with a touch of irony, "So we've met today, Thursday, after all. But of course under very different circumstances."

"Did anyone at the hotel get injured?" her friend inquired.

"No, thank God," Waldo replied. "We came here to see if we could help. I know absolutely nothing about medicine, but Joyce here has had some first-aid training as a flight attendant."

"Thanks so much for coming," said Annette. "We have work for everyone to do."

She then introduced Waldo to a male attendant. "Would you go with Mr. Thomas, please? Perhaps you can help him lift those patients who can't walk."

"Nurse Pierre!" a doctor called from a nearby examining room.

"I'll be right there, sir," she responded. "Joyce and Mandy, you can come with me. I'll be back shortly," she assured Marilyn and Jackie, the other two helpers in their group.

Annette led them into a small cubicle where the physician in charge, Dr. Neville Haynes, was attending to an elderly lady. Her hand had been badly cut by flying glass.

"I've run out of suture material," he advised Annette as they entered. "This wound needs a few more stitches."

Mandy was quickly dispatched to a nurse down the hall and returned with the required supplies. She felt quite involved over the next few hours that they were there as she acted as messenger to the medical team.

Joyce stayed in the room with the doctor, comforting wounded patients. Marilyn and Jackie rolled bandages and dressings salvaged after the storm.

As it neared dusk, Waldo poked his head in.

"I think we'd better be heading back to the hotel," he recommended. "Remember what the manager told us."

Annette reappeared just as they were getting ready to leave.

"Thanks again for all of your help," she said with deep appreciation. "You arrived right when we needed assistance. Bless you all."

"You'll make a fine nurse some day, young lady," Doctor Haynes complimented Mandy. "Other young girls might have been more squeamish. But you really were on the ball."

Mandy smiled with pride as they headed out.

"What a day this has been!" they all agreed later as they munched on sandwiches the chef had prepared for them.

"I just want to get off this island and get back home," mumbled Jackie, irritably. "We can't stay in this sitting room forever."

The manager overheard her and replied, "I guess you haven't heard the latest radio bulletin."

"What did it say?" Marilyn questioned.

"A ham radio operator made contact with another Caribbean radio station. He was told that relief supplies are on their way to us by air from neighboring islands. However, I understand that our airport road is completely blocked by debris. This means that cargo can't get into Roseau, nor can travelers get out, at least not for a while."

"Oh no," Jackie groaned. "I thought we'd be on our way at least by tomorrow."

When night fell, the hotel staff lit the kerosene oil lamps they'd retrieved from a storeroom on the premises. Their flickering flames cast eerie shadows against the stone walls. Mandy watched quietly. The events of the day had come suddenly and were a totally new experience for her. She reflected on the hurricane and its aftermath and wondered what their next move would be.

"I don't know about you folks," Joyce yawned wearily, curling up into a blanket on a couch. "But I'm exhausted. I'll talk more to you all when I awaken."

The next morning a hotel staff member cautioned, "I'd advise you to stay away from the town today. Shops are being looted, especially those that still have food items. A lot of people have nothing to eat."

"It sounds pretty desperate," Mandy admitted to Joyce, privately. "Is there any way in which we can get out and start heading for Barbados?"

"We can't even get a message out to let the folks know we're all right," Joyce conceded gloomily. "The telephone lines are down, and there are no other means of communication at all."

Later that day, they were told that some large cargo vessels had arrived in the harbor, bringing a quantity of relief supplies and some volunteer workers.

"I wonder how long the boats will be here and what will be their next port of call?" Joyce pondered aloud.

"That's it!" cried Waldo, excitedly. "That might be our way of getting out. They might be able to let us aboard and take us with them. Good thinking, Joyce."

New hope and courage surged within the group, as Waldo, Joyce, and Enid went down to the harbor to make inquiries.

Two hours later, the group returned.

"Head for the harbor as quickly as possible!" Waldo shouted. "One of the freighters is sailing this evening, and the captain has promised to take a few passengers aboard, since this is an emergency situation."

A mad scramble ensued. They heartily thanked the hotel's staff, and the group took off toward the wharf.

"How did you manage to convince the captain?" Mandy asked as they waited for orders to board the vessel.

"We were fortunate enough to meet Dr. Haynes while there. He went to receive the medical supplies for the hospital. He seems to be well known in the island and was able to cut through the red tape and plead our case to the captain," Joyce explained.

They breathed a collective sigh of relief when their passports were processed about four o'clock that afternoon and they were allowed aboard. Precariously, they climbed the rope ladder to the upper deck of the ship.

Although the captain wasn't impolite, he addressed them sternly, giving strict orders about his expectations of them while on the ship.

"You will all remain in one area," he warned. "This is not a passenger liner and there are very few sleeping accommodations. We'll be taking a longer route to Barbados, since we've been advised of another storm in the area."

Upon hearing this news, the sixty-odd refugees began to chatter with anxiety. The thought of another hurricane nearby was very frightening.

"Silence!" he commanded. "So far, we are not in any danger. We'll be sailing past St. Lucia and around St. Vincent before landing in Barbados in the morning. We'll be serving you soup and a cold drink a little later. I'm sorry, but that's all we can offer you."

"Sounds great to me," Waldo whispered. "What's important is that we're heading home."

The other teachers in the company were glad to be moving toward Barbados also. They knew that it would be easy for them to get flights from Barbados to their other island destinations. Other tourists caught there during the storm and critically-ill patients from the hospital in Roseau had also been allowed aboard the ship. The plan was to help them get continued treatment in Barbados.

Mandy stood among the gathering as they huddled at the railing, watching the steamer slowly pull away from the harbor. The shoreline receded, becoming a thin, wavy line in the distance. Glancing upward, she observed a large wooden cross still standing on a hilltop. It, obviously, had been untouched by the brutal battering of the winds.

"Thank you, Lord," she whispered to it.

Her faith felt renewed as the liner resolutely began its journey southward.

Passengers climb a rope ladder and board a cargo boat that
will take them away from a hurricane-stricken island.
Photo by Brooks-LaTouche, Barbados.

CHAPTER 8

Browse In Barbados

As the huge freight liner approached Bridgetown Harbor in Barbados early the next morning, Joyce asked the ship's captain, "Do you have a ship-to-shore radio telephone?"

"We do, Ma'am," he replied. "But we only allow the crew to use it."

"Wouldn't you consider this an emergency?" she persisted. "Our relatives don't know we're aboard this ship."

"All right," he agreed, reluctantly. "Please be brief, though."

"Can you guess who this is?" Joyce asked when she was connected to her party.

"Joyce! Where are you?" Keith, her fiancé, asked anxiously. "Oh, thank God you're all right! We were worried sick."

"I'm a grand dame sailing aboard a luxurious ocean liner," she declared. "No kidding, though, at this moment we're pulling into the deepwater harbor aboard a cargo boat. This is the only large vessel in port at the moment that I can observe. Please come as quickly as possible."

Joyce gave him some telephone numbers to call on behalf of a few of the passengers on board.

She also impressed on him the importance of his help in contacting the Barbados Ministry of Health concerning the sick passengers they'd brought with them. "Please tell them that we need a few ambulances also," she advised.

Back on deck, Mandy glanced at her watch. The sun played hide-and-seek behind the wispy clouds that dotted the sky above. Tinges of mauve and scarlet streaked the horizon as dawn fled, giving way to a sparkling new day.

"So this is Barbados at last!" she affirmed. "I don't believe I've ever been so glad to see a place in all my life."

She was so filled with emotion that her voice was scarcely audible. Coming to Barbados was special to her for many reasons. First, she'd finally be able to unwind after the ordeal of the last two days. So much had happened that it seemed more like two years had gone by. Second, Aunt Joyce lives here, so this would be her "home away from home" for the next two weeks. The third reason was a very sentimental one. Barbados was the birthplace of her grand-father, now deceased. Mandy had been very fond of him.

"If Grandpa were alive, he'd be proud to know that I'm here," she declared softly.

"I came from 'Bimshire,'" he used to say. "That name and 'Little England' are the nicknames of my sweet little island home."

He and Mandy's grandmother had met and married in New York after he emigrated from the islands. Their daughters, Joyce and Margaret, Mandy's mother, were both born in New York. It was a pleasant coincidence that Joyce had been sent to live in Barbados by the airline for which she worked—the country that her father had left so long ago.

It felt strange to be on land again after the sixteen-hour voyage from Dominica.

"Keith must have called out the troops," Joyce declared as the passengers disembarked down the gangway.

News reporters and photographers swarmed everywhere. Several ambulances stopped close to shipside to receive the seriously ill passengers, then whisked them off to the hospital.

"Excuse me, Miss. What was it like during the hurricane?" an aggressive reporter questioned, shoving a microphone in Mandy's direction.

She looked quizzically at Joyce.

"Go ahead and give him the story," she encouraged. "We're the first eyewitnesses to arrive here, so they're anxious for an interview. You'll probably see yourself on the television news tonight."

Mandy graciously obliged him, relating her experiences to him and then eagerly greeted Keith. She noticed that his eyes were misty as he and Joyce lovingly embraced.

"I knew from your itinerary that you had to have been there when the storm struck," he said. "But we had no way of contacting you."

Mandy approved of Keith right away. She had longed to meet him after hearing so much about him from her aunt. He was a bachelor of long standing and quite a few years older than Joyce. He had recently risen to the level of manager at a bank in Bridgetown, the capital city.

As Mandy looked him over discreetly, he seemed perfectly matched to Joyce. He was of medium height, muscular, and had a rich dark brown complexion. He seemed capable and energetic while exuding an air of quiet self-confidence.

"God was good to us," Joyce exclaimed. "We've got a lot to tell about the past four weeks."

After parting somewhat sadly from their traveling companions, Keith drove them skillfully up the scenic highway to Joyce's home on the outskirts of the city. She lived in a lovely house in a quiet neighborhood that afforded a marvelous view of the ocean.

"It's great to be home again," she declared, patting the sides of the building.

The hibiscus flowers that lined the perimeter of her tidy miniature garden had unfolded already, as they do every morning, in greeting. Their colors ranged from raging red to dusty rose to tawny beige.

"I want you to know that I faithfully did my duty by this house in your absence," Keith said, jokingly. "The plants are all watered, and you won't find a speck of dust anywhere."

"I'm indeed touched by your acts of kindness," Joyce bantered in reply.

"Please lead me to the bathtub!" begged Mandy. "I want to linger as long as possible in some warm, soapy suds and soak off the grit and grime."

"They're speaking just like Grandpa did," Mandy later exclaimed as she listened to the clipped, almost harsh, rhythmic accent, typical of Barbadians.

Joyce had tuned in to a local radio program. Listeners were invited to call the station and express their views on various issues.

Mandy paid closer attention. The behavior of citizens in public places was the subject under discussion. She was delighted at the figurative speech and colloquialisms that were used with such vigor by the callers.

"The bus stand in town is a case in point," declared one irate woman. "The pushing and shoving gives me the nerves! The police are useless to control those creatures from the animal kingdom. You can't call them human beings."

Mandy laughed uproariously.

"Listen to this next caller," Joyce giggled. "She's describing the people who go, uninvited, to weddings."

"The churches should get security guards to keep them out," the woman proposed. "They only come to be malicious.

Some of them have on as much gold as to pay for an army, and they still aren't behaving decent. Others come looking terrible with their oversized blouses and bad-looking skirts. Yet they're calling at and criticizing the properly-dressed guests."

"I can see that I'm going to thoroughly enjoy my stay here," Mandy gleefully indicated. "I feel right at home."

"Tomorrow we'll go sightseeing," Joyce said. "On the weekend, I'll introduce you to some long-lost relations that I've met since living here."

"Is Keith taking today off?" Mandy asked as Joyce hung up the phone the next morning.

"Yes. He's coming in about an hour's time to take us to Harrison's Cave."

"I think I read a little about that place," Mandy replied. "Am I correct that the cave is located in St. Thomas parish?"

"That's right. The island is divided into eleven districts, called parishes. Ten of them are named after religious saints. The eleventh, Christ Church, is where the airport is located. St. Thomas and St. George are central parishes and are the only ones that don't border on the ocean."

"Harrison's Cave was rediscovered after two hundred years," explained their tour guide, when the threesome boarded the tram-like vehicle later on that day. "A Danish explorer crawled through its damp tunnels and realized that it held extensive rooms and passageways. Other cave explorers, called speleologists, assisted local engineers in developing it into the phenomenon that it is today."

Mandy then experienced perhaps the most exciting and educational underground journey of her life. The mile-long trip took them into areas of unique and unusual beauty. Skillfully placed artificial light sources played on the natural rock formation, creating a feeling of being enclosed in a crystal ice palace.

Mandy learned about stalactites and stalagmites. These refer to coral limestone structures within the cave. The former hang like icicles from the ceiling of the cave. The latter, located opposite on the floor of the cave, rise upward as if to touch them. The carriage rode past hundreds of them of varying lengths and widths.

"Can you hear the sound of rushing water in the background?" Keith asked her as they glided through the semi-darkness.

"I can," she replied. "Is the cave surrounded by water?"

"There are several subterranean streams that flow through here naturally," he explained. "Thousands of gallons of water come in and out daily through the various passages of the cave."

"Look straight ahead now," Joyce urged her. "Isn't this marvelous?"

They had descended to the lowest point of the cave. Their guide invited them to disembark to view a breathtaking waterfall. It plunged into a lighted pool below, and the rushing water glistened as it cascaded downward from its forty-foot height above.

"The trip was far too short," Mandy exclaimed as they emerged thirty minutes later from the depths of the cavern. "I can never really describe for the folks back home what it's like."

"The combination of artistic genius, engineering skills, and hard work that it took to make it a tourist attraction is really amazing," Joyce remarked.

"How about a jaunt to Bathsheba?" Keith suggested. "Mandy, you seem to be in the mood for 'things different' today."

He drove them off the beaten path through the Barbados countryside. The network of roads was well sign-posted through hundreds of acres of sugar cane fields.

"Sugar is king in this island," Joyce declared, pointing out the young green plants under cultivation. "The harvesting season extends from February to June each year, after which we have the popular 'Cropover' festival."

"Is that like Carnival?" Mandy asked.

"Yes. It's almost as explosive as what you witnessed in Antigua," laughed Keith. "We have our own lively version of calypsos, steel bands, and parades also."

The pounding surf of the Atlantic Ocean was fully in view as the narrow road that they were on took them toward it. They passed through several quaint rural villages, each containing clusters of wooden chattel houses perched at various distances from the roadside. Chickens squawked lustily as they passed. Barefooted and bare-bottomed children darted in and out of their homes. Locally-bred black-bellied sheep grazed contently. Mandy learned that this is a special breed of sheep, very common in Barbados, which has no wool. Heavily-laden fruit trees, such as coconut, breadfruit, and mango abounded.

The road wound and descended as they drove further, eventually becoming a flat, well-paved highway along the seacoast.

"This is our famous East Coast Road," Joyce explained. "We're on the opposite side of the island from where we began."

The view was magnificent as they moved along the coastline. The white-capped breakers rushed furiously toward the shore. Adventurous surfboarders dangerously rode the crests of the waves. Seagrapes bent low and grew in wild abandon. They struck a rugged contrast to the stately cabbagenut palm trees neatly planted along the sandy shore. The strong, salty sea breezes whirled, lashing their faces, but that did not disturb the peaceful solitude that engulfed them.

They came upon an interesting sight as they moved further along. Gigantic coral boulders in the water formed an irregular arc, stretching one-half mile along the edges of the ocean. As if deposited there by nature's own hand, the boulders stood in majestic beauty, solid and timeless.

The threesome lunched on the terrace of a small hotel in the area, popular for its local cuisine. From there, Mandy noticed a fleet of interestingly decorated fishing boats anchored nearby. Painted on their sides were witty names, mostly female, like "Lady Lu," "Princess Anne," and "Black Pearl."

"What time do the boats go out?" she asked, noticing the fishermen washing their nets.

"That's a question for Keith," Joyce replied. "He goes fishing several times a year."

The winding rural road to the seacoast of Bathsheba
on the eastern side of Barbados.
Photo by Leonard Higginson, New York, N.Y.

"The boats can leave at any hour of the day or night, especially for deep sea fishing. I don't have time to go out much anymore, but I've always gone late at night when it's cooler."

"It must be an eerie feeling to be surrounded by the ocean in just a small vessel," said Mandy.

"Yes," Keith agreed. "But reaching the barrier reef a few miles out, dropping anchor and hauling in the catch of bonitas, billfish, and dolphin is really an exciting experience."

After lunch they poked around in a magnificent public garden nearby. It contained thousands of tropical plants and flowers, beautifully arranged amid natural rocks and cascading streams.

"This island tour wouldn't be complete," Keith advised, "without a visit to the renowned Sam Lord's Castle."

"Was Sam Lord the famous pirate that my Grandpa told me about?" asked Mandy, "The one who instigated several shipwrecks and plundered their cargoes?"

"That's correct," Joyce confirmed. "Legend has it that the nineteenth century bandit hung lanterns in coconut trees inland in order to fool passing ships at night. The idea was to trick them into believing that they were near the island's harbor."

"Naturally," Keith continued, "the ships ran aground on the surrounding rocks. Old Sam killed off any crew that survived and became quite wealthy from the loot. That was how he was able to build his castle."

Leaving the parish of St. Joseph, the travelers meandered through St. John and into St. Philip, where they found the Castle. As they entered the grounds, Mandy noticed that the area had been transformed into a luxury hotel resort. The architects had kept the original façade. However, the inside of the elegant new building was adorned tastefully with antique furniture and artifacts.

They strolled past lovely fountains and well-kept lawns, following a winding footpath that descended to the beach below. The sky was an explosion of orange as dusk approached that late afternoon.

"Nothing can surpass these Caribbean sunsets," Joyce said as they lingered awhile there then wended their way back home.

They found Cousin Kit the next Saturday afternoon humming contentedly in her rocking chair. She sat on the verandah of the house she'd lived in for over one-half century. Joyce had phoned ahead to advise her that they would be coming by to see her. Eagerly awaiting their visit, Cousin Kit donned her best apron and head wrap. Her house was located in a small rural village in the northern parish of St. Peter.

As Mandy glanced around at the spotlessly clean dwelling, Joyce asked her, "Not bad for a young lady of ninety-eight years, is it?"

Cousin Kit's modest home was filled with mementos from the past. Its walls displayed faded photographs of persons whom the aging lady had known or admired over the years. A three-legged antique mahogany table occupied a corner all by itself. On it were a number of greeting cards from persons held dear.

Joyce stared at a shiny black old hand-operated sewing machine.

"Does this still work, Cousin Kit?" she inquired.

"Indeed it does," she emphatically replied. "I bought it about sixty years ago. I'm a seamstress by profession, you know. Mrs. Keturah Waterman is my name. I made the dresses for many a bride in my day. I still make my own clothing and my curtains even now."

Mandy had been informed that Cousin Kit was her oldest living relative. But it was hard to believe that this sprightly little woman, who wore neither eyeglasses, dentures, nor hearing aids, and whose memory was so remarkable, could really be that old.

"What's the secret to your long life, Cousin Kit?" asked Mandy.

"'Trust in the Lord with all thine heart and lean not unto thine own understanding. In all thy ways acknowledge Him and He shall direct thy paths,'" she quoted from the Bible. "That's my motto and the secret of my success in life."

Mandy and Joyce sat entranced as their elderly relative took them back in time and unfolded for them information about their Barbadian heritage.

"I remember when your grandfather was born, Mandy," she told her. "He was the oldest of my Dear Aunt's children. A sturdy little baby and a mischievous lad he was," she chuckled. "When I was growing up," she explained,

"We called our oldest aunt or our most cherished aunt, 'Dear Aunt.' That title let them and everyone know that we greatly respected and loved that person. I really enjoyed being around and helping my Dear Aunt."

Mandy listened, quietly imbibing all that she said. Some of the tales were quite humorous, others more serious. She even sprinkled in a few family secrets! But, as she gazed into that ancient, wrinkle-free face, Mandy felt deeply gratified and touched by the experience of meeting Cousin Kit. It was as if missing pieces to a vital family puzzle had now shifted into place.

"This trip to meet you has meant more to me than you'll ever know, Cousin Kit," she acknowledged as they embraced her before leaving.

By the end of her stay in Barbados, Mandy understood why it had been dubbed "Little England." She discovered that this pear-shaped island, densely populated by those of African descent and sitting far easterly in the ocean, has a lifestyle as British as they come. Further, it has been this way since the first settlers landed there in the early 1600s and Bajans (short for Barbadians) are extremely proud of this fact. Mandy saw and felt the British influence everywhere, from the traffic moving on the left side of the road to lawyers wearing white wigs at the high courts of law. Mandy learned first-hand while there that, not surprisingly, the main religious denomination is called the "Church of England."

"I've been attending an Anglican church since moving to Barbados," Joyce explained as Mandy accompanied her to church the following Sunday. "In the US it's called the Episcopal faith."

This proved to be an entirely new experience for Mandy. The style of worship was very formal, the atmosphere hushed and somewhat restrained. Her church services back home in New York were much more relaxed like Reverend Christian's in St. Thomas.

The church building was quite ornate, adorned with materials imported from England generations before. A white-carved scroll was stretched along one wall of the sanctuary. The words of a Psalm were affixed to it. The marble flooring and the ceiling overhead bore lovely floral designs. A large wooden crucifix hung high over the altar. Circular white pillars were placed throughout the edifice. A heavy, round, dark wooden pulpit, from which the priest delivered his sermons, was located at the front.

The sexton tolled the bell, inviting worshippers to enter. The pews quickly filled as the organ pealed forth the sacred melodies.

Joyce pressed a small black book into her niece's hand. It was the English Hymnal, containing the Hymns Ancient and Modern, prayers, and psalms. It helped her follow the service.

Mandy watched, intrigued, at the procession that moved up the center aisle. At the head of the line were three young men, called acolytes, with pious expressions on their faces. Their manner of dress was so unusual. They wore long-sleeved, ankle-length red coats, called cassocks, over which were white blouse-like shirts called cottas. Each carried a long wooden pole. At the top of the center pole was a crucifix. Lighted candles crowned the ones on either side. An all-male choir followed, lustily singing the old hymn, "Now Thank We All Our God." Their attire was different from the acolytes' and consisted of white full-sleeved surplices under which were dark blue cassocks. Mandy was impressed by the very young choir boys who appeared to be no older than nine or ten years old. Their high-pitched voices sweetly carried the melody. They were dressed like the older men, but in addition, their necks were encircled by high-standing white pleated collarettes. Upon approaching the chancel at the front, the young men genuflected before the altar and took their places in their stalls.

The priest emerged from a side office, called a vestry, and entered the sanctuary. He also wore vestments in the old English tradition comprising cassock, alb, surplice, and chasuble. As he approached the altar, two acolytes, called the thurifer and the boat boy, brought him incense with which to bless the altar. As it was lighted, the smoke curled upward. Mandy smelled the sweet fragrance that pervaded the air.

The mass continued with the priest intoning psalms and prayers. The congregation accepted these offerings to God by interspersing their responses in song. Mandy took time while there to thank God for His help on the tour thus far. She was especially grateful for His protection over them during their ordeal in the Dominica hurricane.

Keith, a devout Methodist, picked them up after his service and drove them to his parents' home for lunch. The couple, Elmira and Courtney Brathwaite, lived in the parish of Christ Church, about four miles from Bridgetown. They were typical middle-class Barbadians who were nearing retirement age. Their comfortable house bore a name that had some significance like most houses do in Barbados. Theirs was called "Elm's Court," cleverly named after them.

Mr. and Mrs. Brathwaite were looking forward, with great anticipation, to Joyce's and Keith's wedding. They got along splendidly with her and welcomed her and Mandy heartily when they arrived.

"Come right in," urged Mrs. Brathwaite, offering them drinks as they entered.

The aroma of cooking filled the air. Lashley, their maid, clothed in a clean blue uniform with a white lace cap and apron, greeted them warmly from the kitchen.

When Mandy pulled herself away from the table, she felt completely full.

"I think you introduced me to the best in Barbadian cooking all in one day," she told their hostess.

Lashley had outdone herself with the excellent meal. The menu consisted of baked chicken with gravy, fried flying fish (a fish especially abundant in the sea off Barbados), pigeon peas and rice, pickled breadfruit, plantain fritters, black pudding (a sausage-like delicacy), and cold marinated pork called "souse."

For dessert, Mrs. Brathwaite herself had specially baked her unsurpassed Bajan fruitcake. They washed it all down with a punch made from a blend of tropical fruit.

"Are flying fish caught on a line?" Mandy asked.

"No, my dear," Mr. Brathwaite responded. "The fishermen catch them in nets not very far out from the shore. They invade our waters each year from November to June."

"Fish sellers peddle them on the wharf and in the markets when they're in season," Keith injected. "Local industries freeze them to make them available all year round."

"I heard my grandfather speak often of 'flying fish and cuckoo,'" laughed Mandy. "He used to say it was his favorite meal on Saturday evenings when he was a boy."

Lashley showed Mandy a flat wooden stick. She explained that the 'cuckoo stick,' as it's called, is used to blend cuckoo, a thick, savory, porridge-like dish. It's is made from yellow cornmeal mixed with finely chopped okras. Various types of seasonings are blended in.

"I've discovered that it's a favorite of most Bajans," Joyce told her. "You can call it the national dish."

Over the next few days, Mandy experienced snatches of how the local inhabitants lived. This is what she had hoped for.

The sidewalks of Broad Street, the main shopping thoroughfare, were hardly wide enough to contain the mass of people who converged in Bridgetown. Joyce parked the car in Independence Square before commencing their walking tour. They paused on the pedestrian walk of the Chamberlain Bridge before moving to the top of the town. Mandy viewed the picturesque Careenage, or seaside enclave, where fishing boats and small sailing vessels were moored. She took several snapshots of Trafalgar Square, the Treasury Building, and the Public Buildings where Parliament meets.

One of Joyce's friends greeted her.

"It's always like this," Joyce chuckled. "I never come to Bridgetown without meeting at least a half dozen people I know. It's hard to remain anonymous in a small island like this."

"This must have been quite a change for you, Aunt Joyce, coming from the independent lifestyle of New York."

"In some ways, it's been a pleasant change," Joyce mused. "A friend is never far away. There are times, of course, when I'd prefer a little privacy. But, an island is really a big, small town."

Mandy noticed when they exchanged their money at the bank, that, as in other islands, local currency was used. Instead of the jade green color of the US notes, each denomination was a different color. Except for the seven-sided silver dollar, the coins were similar to those back home.

"I'm going to browse a little by myself while you take care of business," Mandy indicated.

"That's fine," Joyce approved. "Don't stray too far from Broad Street, although you really can't get lost."

The stores and shops of Bridgetown were favorite haunts for passengers from the large ocean liners, just as they were in Nassau and Charlotte Amalie. The tourists joined the throngs of Bajans in quest of the latest bargains.

As Mandy rode the elevators and escalators of the large department stores, she saw a wide assortment of local and imported merchandise on the counters.

Colorful fishing vessels are moored in the Careenage off the deepwater harbor in Bridgetown, Barbados.
Photo by Leonard Higginson, New York, N.Y.

She forayed into the side streets and alleyways of the town and discovered that they were small communities in themselves. She smiled at their colorful names like "Amen Alley," "Milk Market," and "Lakes Folly." The ever-present vendors, here in Barbados called "hawkers," did major business there. They sold either packaged nuts, sugar cakes and candies called "sweets," or fruit in season, such as ackees, mangoes and oranges. Small shops in these lanes carried items not always available in the larger stores and supermarkets. Customers' purchases ranged from home remedies for aches and pains to seasonings and spices for cooking.

"This is mauby bark," an obliging hawker informed her, pointing to some dried brown strips tied in small bundles in her tray.

Mandy had heard of it and asked her, "Doesn't that have a bitter taste?"

The woman took time to explain, "You add water, orange peel, and cloves to it and boil it. When it cools down, you add sugar and ice for a long, refreshing drink that's 'too sweet' for your thirst."

Mandy chatted with her for a while and then asked her permission to take a photograph. The vendor flashed a broad, toothless grin, smoothed her patchwork apron, and lifted her tray to her head for a charming pose. Mandy, giggling to herself, thanked her heartily and moved on.

She noticed as she meandered further that an array of other services was available in these narrow byways as well. Hairdressers, barber shops, shoemakers, and small jewelry establishments thrived, bringing much-needed incomes to their owners.

"There you are," called Joyce some hours later.

All the way home, Mandy jabbered about her morning's exploration.

"I think you could easily live here," her aunt observed. "You seemed to have fit right in with the people."

No sooner than Joyce had entered her driveway, a policeman on a motorcycle pulled in behind her. He was smartly uniformed in a short-sleeved, open-neck white tunic with shiny silver buttons on the lapels and down the front. A brown leather belt encircled his waist. His navy blue trousers had a bright red stripe down either side. His feet were hidden in highly polished black boots. He wore a white-peaked helmet on his head with the word POLICE painted across it. He was not dressed like the ordinary policemen who patrolled the streets of Bridgetown.

Joyce, rather concerned, addressed him, "May I help you, Officer?"

"Is this where Miss Joyce Rosewell lives?" he inquired.

She answered him affirmatively.

"I have been asked to deliver this envelope to you," he announced, handing it to her. Then, as quickly as he came, he rode off in the distance.

Joyce quickly tore open the envelope, and then breathed more easily after scanning its contents.

"We're invited to a reception at Government House next week in honor of a visiting African Head of State," she informed.

"*We* are invited? Who would have known I'm here?" Mandy asked, exceedingly pleased.

Joyce, laughing, winked at her. "Someone who knew you'd want to attend. No kidding, though, I believe Keith must have helped make it possible."

The telephone rang as they went inside. It was Kathy Kirton, a friend of Joyce's, calling. Kathy was the host of "Coffee Time," a daily radio variety program. Interesting people from interesting places were guests on her broadcast.

"Hi Joyce, I hear you had a harrowing experience in Dominica," she exclaimed. "I'd like to interview you about it one morning soon."

"I wouldn't mind at all. But, better still, why not let my niece, Amanda, who was there with me, tell you all about it? We've been on a tour through the islands this summer."

"Great," replied Kathy. "How about Thursday morning?"

Mandy, who'd overheard their conversation, answered, "It's a date."

Mandy tried to remember the things that had happened in Dominica. She could almost hear the terrifying sound of the wind again as it ripped through the island. Visions of that hectic scene at the hospital with the many injured people came rushing back. By Thursday, she was ready to recount these for Kathy's listeners.

Mandy rode alone on the colorful blue-and-gold public bus to the radio station. She learned that these were the national colors, adopted since 1966, when the island became independent. They were the major colors of the flag as well. She deposited her fare in the coin box, and a conductress indicated a seat near the front to her. A full-bosomed, ample woman across the aisle avidly munched on some peanuts. Two elderly gentlemen at the rear were engrossed loudly in a discussion. Their opinions brought chuckles from the other passengers. Hawkers with heavy baskets laden with produced from the countryside rode to the market in town also.

Mandy waited for Kathy near the information desk of the broadcasting studio as agreed. She observed a rush of activity around Kathy. Snatches of music floated out to the hallway from a door marked "Studio A." A group of bouncing, pushing children from a summer day camp was also visiting that morning. Their youthful teacher tried rather unsuccessfully to keep them together. A newscaster dashed past with a sheaf of papers in his hand. When Kathy welcomed her into the studio, she was surprised to see how compact it was. Mandy felt a wee bit nervous as she entered the closed-in, high-ceilinged, circular room. It was rather bare and had no windows. Kathy offered her a cup of coffee and showed her to a seat beside her at a table with a microphone in the middle. Mandy's heart sank for a moment when she saw it. She considered the vast audience that, no doubt, would be listening and hoped her voice would not betray her anxiety.

They chatted awhile before going on the air for the live broadcast. Kathy was so warm and reassuring that Mandy forgot for a moment that she was almost 'on stage.'

She glanced toward the mezzanine overhead and glimpsed the recording paraphernalia behind the thick glass window. The engineer signaled that they were about to begin. A green light flashed and they were on.

Kathy conversed with her listeners in the rich, assured voice of the professional that she was.

"Here we are at 'Kathy's Coffee Time' again," she welcomed them. "In our studio this morning is Miss Amanda Rivers, a teenaged student from New York City. She is with us today to share with us a snapshot of her recent harrowing experience in Dominica. Most of us are aware, of course, that our neighboring isle was stricken by a giant hurricane. Amanda, our guest, was present there at the time, riding out the storm. Tell us, Amanda, what was the most unforgettable part of your experience?"

Mandy, now at ease, clearly and animatedly recalled those frightful moments. Before she knew it, time was up and the interview was over.

"You were terrific," Joyce greeted her when she got back home. "Listen for yourself."

To her pleasant surprise, her aunt had tape recorded the program, which provided her a precious memento to take back home.

Mandy found out that a trip to the beach is a popular event for both locals and tourists alike in Barbados. Many people take 'sea baths,' as they call them, early in the morning before going to work. She and Joyce spent one lazy afternoon at a beautiful beach nearby. Vendors shaded themselves from the sizzling sun under thatched-roofed, open-sided huts. Among their items for sale were coconut and tortoise-shell jewelry and boldly-printed sundresses and tropical shirts. Mandy bought a few souvenirs from them to take back home.

As she sat on the beach making circles with her feet in the sand, Mandy observed that water sports are a big attraction here. Agile young men commanded catamarans with tall, full sails, urging sun-tanned visitors to climb aboard. Water skiers, clad in life jackets, skillfully glided over the glistening waves. Their hands clung firmly to ropes, which attached them to the rear of motorboats.

Mandy eagerly joined a group for a ride in a glass-bottomed boat. The boat captain and guide pointed out relics of ancient shipwrecks as well as a variety of fish.

Mandy wanted to know more about the shipwrecks and questioned him further.

He advised her, "Although Barbados was not discovered by Christopher Columbus, as most of the other islands were, it was still along the sea route of the treasure ships that plied the waters between here and Europe. Many a ship was wrecked on the surrounding reefs, and several were overtaken by seafaring pirates and buccaneers."

Fascinated, Mandy decided that upon her return home she would delve still further into the colorful history of these islands.

The reception on the grounds of the Governor's mansion was truly a gala affair. Among the invited guests were government officials, senior civil servants, and persons from the upper echelons of society. Mandy wore the garment created for her by Madame St. Jacques of Haiti. It was perfect for the occasion. Joyce was most attractive in a floor-length, black-sequined, two-piece outfit.

"You both look incredibly stunning," Keith assured them as they approached the lovely grounds.

When they presented their invitations, they were granted entrance into the highly prestigious gathering. They promenaded through the manicured gardens and were met by members of the receiving line. Mandy smiled graciously, shaking hands with the dignitaries.

The visiting African Prime Minister, in whose honor the party was held, arrived by private jet, along with a contingent of aides and ladies in waiting. They were dazzling in the rainbow of colors of their splendid national dress. Some of the women wore their hair braided high into intricate patterns. Others wore beautifully-wrapped turbans that complemented their attire.

Joyce discreetly pointed out to Mandy the "Who's Who" of Barbadian society. There were only a few young people present, but Mandy was thrilled to have been included among such a distinguished crowd.

The hostesses moved deftly among the guests, offering exquisitely prepared delicacies. Mandy spoke with a few of the African women who were among the visiting delegation. They exchanged a host of interesting and worthwhile information from their respective parts of the world. For example, Mandy asked them questions about the role of girls and women in their country. She wanted to know if girls and boys have equal educational opportunities, and if women can be elected to government positions. They answered Mandy's questions forthrightly, and, Mandy gave them answers to their questions about fashion and music trends in America.

The two-week rendezvous in Barbados ended before Mandy realized it.

"I can't believe our vacation is nearly over, Aunt Joyce," she lamented. "We've only a few more days to go."

"You'll enjoy the remaining places we'll visit, though," Joyce assured her. "The Grenadines will be a pleasant change. Also, you'll find that Curaçao, a Dutch West Indian Island, and Trinidad are distinctly different from the places we've been to already."

So passport and tickets in hand, the adventurers were off again for the final leg of their journey.

CHAPTER 9

Gliding Among The Grenadines

Recalling their journey to Barbados aboard the freight liner, Mandy declared, "This is certainly a big improvement over the last ship we were on, Aunt Joyce."

"After that experience, I never thought I'd ever want to get on board another boat," her Aunt replied. "But here we are again and enjoying it."

They were sailing toward the Grenadines on a small fifty-passenger cruise liner. They were sharing a cabin for their three-day, laid-back junket aboard this vessel. They'd left Barbados for St. Vincent the day before in a small propeller aircraft. After a day of shopping there, they'd boarded the ship, anticipating the fun-filled hours that awaited them.

"Comprising one hundred or more islands and cays, the Grenadines sit like tiny pearls in the ocean. They stretch seventy miles between St. Vincent to the north and

Grenada at their southern end," their captain explained as they floated on the crystal clear sea. "St. Vincent and Grenada are each responsible for administering these lush island hideaways. Many of them are uninhabited. However, some of them are the vacation playgrounds for the British Royal Family."

Aboard the ship, the passengers were casually dressed and thoroughly enjoying themselves among all of the activities and the shipboard barbeques. They were nearly all American or European tourists.

Mandy recalled that the Joseph family they'd met in Tortola hailed from the island of St. Vincent. She thought it would have been fun to have them here with them. She'd learned a lot about St. Vincent and this region from them. For example, they told her that St. Vincent is a small nation of 92,000 people and is a major source of arrowroot for many world markets. It's a crop from which many products, such as baby food, are made.

She'd also gleaned a lot about Grenada. Located ninety miles north of Trinidad, it's a lovely land of mountains and valleys, familiarly known as the "Spice Island," because of its wide cultivation of nutmeg, cloves, and cinnamon, among other spices. Grenada's famous Grand Anse Beach is rated among the finest in the Caribbean.

The ship docked at two remote tranquil islands by day, allowing the passengers to relax on the powdery-white sandy beaches. The snorkelers and divers were in their own mini-paradise because the surrounding reefs teemed with exotic underwater sea life. They sailed again in the evenings, enjoying the tropical night breezes from the trade winds.

Their first port of call was Palm Island, a 110-acre cay in the center of that island chain. Several small vessels and private yachts were noted in its environs. The passengers were ferried to a small cottage resort where a marvelous seafood lunch was served. In the distance, Mandy could sight neighboring Union Island.

Their second stop was Mustique, an island filled with palm groves and green valleys.

Its coastline was only twelve miles long.

"It seems as if this is largely an agricultural island," Joyce observed as they did some sightseeing there.

An elderly farmer that they met, clarified, "When we harvest our citrus fruit, it is first sent to St. Vincent. From there it is shipped on to other island territories. We raise and eat our own poultry and cattle."

Their third and final day was spent entirely aboard the ship. They sailed southward near to Carriacou, an island owned by Grenada, the largest of this group. Although not disembarking, they anchored briefly off Petit St. Vincent. They later passed Petit Martinique and then made their way back toward St. Vincent.

As evening approached they could see Bequia, the largest of St. Vincent's satellites. They were near enough to view the colorful tropical foliage and the scenic mountaintop terrain.

At the end of this marvelous floating holiday, the passengers hugged one another and then went their separate ways. Joyce and Mandy stayed overnight at a hotel in Kingstown, St. Vincent's capital.

"We have to be up at the crack of dawn, young lady, to take our flight to Trinidad," Joyce reminded. "So enjoy your beauty rest. I'll call you in the morn."

CHAPTER 10

Traipsing In Trinidad

"What a contrast to the calm and quiet of the Grenadines!" remarked Mandy as they drifted through throbbing, thumping Frederick Street.

They were in the heart of Port of Spain, Trinidad's fast-paced cosmopolitan capital. As was the case in many of the other islands they visited, Joyce was familiar with this major city because of her airline stopovers. However, for the first time she was enjoying other attractions and places of interest in these islands on this exciting excursion with Mandy.

While traipsing through the town making purchases, they were enveloped by the lunchtime crowd that emerged from office buildings. The shops and restaurants in the area were jammed with people. They paused on a bench to rest a while in nearby Woodford Square.

Mandy reflected on her first impression upon landing in this nation of one million people.

"If you've seen Trinidad, you've seen the world," she said.

She realized that this island was by far the most varied in religions, races, cultures, customs, and cuisine, than any in the Caribbean.

"Angela should be here shortly," Joyce stated. "She said she'd meet us around noon."

Angela Singh, a close friend of Joyce's with whom they were staying in Trinidad, was a lawyer. She practiced in Port of Spain but lived in Arima, the island's third largest town. It was near Piarco International Airport and also near the campus of the University of the West Indies, a branch campus of the ones in Jamaica and Barbados.

While waiting for Angela, they thought it would be fun to quietly "people-watch."

Mandy had been told that the descendants of Africans, Indians, Chinese, Syrians, South Americans, and Europeans, each with their distinctive lifestyles, comprise the population of this so-called "Caribbean melting pot." The wonderful mix of people that passed, indeed, bore testimony to this. The shapes of eyes, the languages spoken, the range of hair textures, the body movements, and styles of clothing were diverse, yet intricately bound together in the fabric of this society.

A knot of ebony-hued youth trotted past. One carried a mammoth transistor radio on his shoulder that blared forth a popular calypso tune. The others snapped their fingers and bobbed in step to the catchy, pulsating beat. They saw blondes, brunettes, shirt-jacketed men, and others of European extraction. They were remnants, no doubt, of the nation's former planter class that thrived in colonial days.

Two restless, squealing children caught their attention. The two were obviously exhausted from their shopping expedition in the sweltering midday heat, and their young parents were having considerable difficulty keeping them in tow. Their father, lean and lanky, wore an open shirt and sported a short-cropped Afro hairstyle. Their mother had strong Chinese features, was tiny in build, and had black straight hair. The children were charmingly, but very differently, endowed with their parents' racial heritages. Each had the high cheekbones and almond-shaped eyes of their mother. But there the similarity to each other ended. Except for the marvelous riot of bushy hair on his head, the boy might have been a replica of his mother. He was petite, small-boned, and fair skinned. The little girl, however, received a greater share of her father's features. She was tall, bronze-colored, and a mass of thick black curls rimmed her face.

Angela joined them just then. She was tall and slender, olive-skinned, and very attractive. Her appearance was typical of her Indian ancestry.

"Sorry to be late," she apologized. "I'm free, though, for the rest of the day, and I'll be taking tomorrow off from work. How's your day going so far?"

They walked to the other end of Frederick Street where the well-known Queen's Park Savannah is located. This nearly 200-acre green pastureland, they discovered, is head-quarters for many national activities.

"Our major football and hockey matches, as well as our carnival parades, are held here," Angela informed. "It's the site for our horse racing meets as well."

"What about cricket?" Joyce inquired.

"That's played in another section of the city at the Queen's Park Oval."

Mandy glanced around the open Savannah. Vendors peddling oysters, coconuts, and roasted corn were every-where. A few joggers made laps around the three-mile cir-cumference.

"Everything really does go on here, doesn't it?" Joyce laughed.

Mandy noticed that the buildings bordering the area were a hodge-podge of architectural designs. The gothic Anglican Cathedral was located there as well as old colo-nial mansions. French, and Mediterranean-styled office buildings that housed foreign embassies were scattered in between. North of the Savannah was the President's official residence, which bordered the Botanic Gardens.

"Our nation didn't planned very well how to separate, appropriately, our commercial, domestic, and social build-ings, did we?" chuckled Angela.

They browsed a while in the lovely Botanic Gardens where shady royal palm trees stood. There were also many varieties of plants and brilliant tropical flowers there in natural sloping arrangements.

"Did you know that Trinidad was once a part of the South American continent?" Angela asked.

"Really?" replied Mandy, rather surprised.

"I know that it's only nine miles from here to Venezuela," Joyce injected. "But I didn't realize that they were once connected."

"The geologists tell us that the areas became detached millions of years ago," Angela continued. "Apparently, that's the reason why our plants and animals are more like those of our southern neighbors."

Mandy, interested, quizzed her further, "What plants and animals are here that are different from those found in other Caribbean islands?"

"We have armadillos, raccoons, deer, and alligators. In our mountain forests, there are ocelots, from the tiger family, and snakes, also."

"Speaking of animals," Joyce proposed, "we're looking forward to visiting Caroni Bird Sanctuary. Every book that you read about Trinidad mentions it."

"Let's plan to visit there tomorrow then," Angela proposed as they drove homeward. "It's fairly close to where I live."

"What's that elaborate building over there?" Mandy asked, as they passed through a section called St. James.

"That's a Muslim mosque," Angela advised. "There are several of them as well as Hindu temples throughout the country."

The large, white-domed green-and-white structure was immaculately clean on the outside and highly ornate.

Joyce remarked, "I'm told that thousands of people here follow the Hindu and Muslim religions."

"That's right. Many years ago when East Indians were recruited here as indentured laborers, they brought along their customs and religions, of course."

"What other religions are practiced here?" Mandy inquired.

"Roman Catholic, Anglican, Pentecostal, Presbyterian, and other Protestant denominations are the major ones."

"I passed through Trinidad once in late October," Joyce said. "I learned that the Hindus were commemorating an important ancient festival and it was therefore a public holiday."

"It must have been Divali, the Festival of Lights," Angela explained. "A Hindu friend once told me the long story behind it. Essentially, it symbolizes the triumph of light, representing good, over darkness, denoting evil."

Mandy asked about the Muslim festivals.

"There are several throughout the year. March is usually the month for Husain, which commemorates the death of one of Mohammed's descendants."

Joyce exclaimed, "Angela, we've repeatedly remarked on how much of an education we're getting on this tour. We've already decided that we'll compare notes and write about our experiences."

Angela lived with her parents in Arima, a densely populated town. It's located at the foot of a mountain range that stretches across the northern end of the island. Their large, comfortable, two-story wooden house was surrounded by fruit trees. Several coconut trees stood in the back garden, and smaller lime and guava trees were nearby.

Mr. and Mrs. Singh had migrated to Trinidad from Guyana several years before. Mr. Singh was very proud of his country of origin and loved to explain to visitors about it.

"Guyana is a country in South America. It borders on Surinam, where Dutch is spoken, Venezuela, and Brazil."

"I must warn you guys that Daddy's on a roll with his Guyanese history lesson," Angela laughed.

Mr. Singh only smiled and continued, "Although Guyana is located on the South American continent, its culture and history are more like those of the Caribbean Islands. In fact, having once been a British colony, it's considered to be a part of the English-speaking Caribbean."

"I've only been in-transit there at the airport," Joyce said. "However, I've often heard my Guyanese friends talk about the three large rivers over there. If I recall correctly, they're the Essequibo, Berbice, and Demerara Rivers, aren't they?"

"You're exactly right," Mrs. Singh injected. "There are two other interesting things about Guyana. Like Jamaica, bauxite is an important natural resource. Second, it's similar to Trinidad in that the population there is largely of Indian and African descent."

"I might as well join this conversation," Angela stated. "Although I was born here in Trinidad, I visited Guyana many times as I was growing up, so I know a lot about it. It has a huge interior hinterland, but most of the people live along the coast and in the capital, Georgetown."

"It sounds like a fascinating place," Mandy said. "What made your family come to Trinidad?"

"Daddy was a young apprentice in the sugar industry. He liked what he saw on a visit here, and they transferred him here permanently."

"Our two older children were born in Guyana," his wife informed. "Angela is our only Trinidadian."

"And what an illustrious Trinidadian she is!" Joyce exclaimed. "She seems to be making her mark in the law courts here from what I understand."

That night, Angela hosted a dinner party in honor of her houseguests. Mandy thoroughly enjoyed the evening as she mingled with those invited. Among the guests were included the younger members of an Amerindian family next door. Many learned that Amerindians are descendants of the original island inhabitants. Other dinner guests were Teasley Alleyne, a prominent dentist, and Daisy Wilson, a lively nurse. Oudit Samaroo, Angela's "special guy," who Joyce had met previously, was also in the group. Kenneth and Gladys Chin, a couple from Tobago, Trinidad's sister island, completed the jovial gathering.

Oudit was the life of the party and kept them laughing throughout the evening. His personality was rather opposite Angela's quiet, almost taciturn, nature. He managed a chain of jewelry stores in Port-of-Spain and was becoming quite successful at it.

Mandy was introduced to a splendid Indian meal that evening. Various kinds of curried meats, such as chicken, shrimp, and beef were included. Dhal, a split peas soup served with rice, was also on the menu. Joyce especially enjoyed the variety of fresh vegetables prepared hot and spicy. Curried mango and fried pumpkin were among them.

Paratha, a type of roti, was also served. Unlike other types of roti, paratha is light and flaky and doesn't contain meat. Mrs. Singh explained to Mandy about other kinds of roti. "One popular type is sold in restaurants and by street vendors. It is usually eaten by itself as a quick meal. Its ingredients include curried meat, split peas, potatoes, seasonings and spices. These are wrapped in a thin dough, called a skin, baked previously on a hot griddle stone, called a tawa. You should try it before you leave Trinidad. I'm sure you'll like it," she said.

The meal ended with an assortment of Indian sweets served for desert. These were complemented by a refreshing beverage of fresh coconut water from the garden trees.

"Have you been to our famous Pitch Lake yet?" Kenneth asked the guests of honor.

"We hope to go there on Friday," Mandy replied.

Teasley advised, "I have some business to take care of in San Fernando on Friday. La Brea, where the Lake is located, is about twenty miles further. But I'd be happy to take you there. We can return here to Arima by evening."

"That would be great," Joyce readily accepted. "What time should we be ready?"

"We should get started about seven a.m."

"Will you be attending Charles's and Sandra's wedding on Saturday, Angela?" Daisy inquired.

"You know I have to," she replied. "They'd never forgive me if I didn't. In fact, Sandra knew that I was having house guests, so she told me that Mandy and Joyce are also invited to the wedding."

"I'm looking forward to it," Mandy affirmed.

The party broke up around midnight. As they departed, the Chins promised to see them all at the wedding.

When Mandy snuggled into bed that night, she heard the grating chorus of the tropical night creatures to which she was finally getting accustomed. It took her a while to appreciate that the toads, frogs, crickets, and other insects made a glorious symphony all their own.

Late the following afternoon, the three young women boarded the flat-bottomed boat that took them into the famous Caroni Bird Sanctuary.

"We have a tremendous bird population here," Angela informed. "I'm told that there are over four hundred species."

"Isn't this island known as the "Land of the Hummingbird?" asked Joyce.

Their guide interjected, "That's right. In fact, we have about eighteen different species of those tiny, rapidly flying creatures. They come in a multitude of colors."

The ride in the cool of the day through the 10,000-acre wilderness was truly a pleasant experience. They slowly negotiated the narrow channels through thick, muddy water. The guide pointed out as many swamp creatures as he could see, including ducks, herons, parrots, lizards, shellfish, and fur-bearing animals as well as flocks of white egrets.

The visitors were certainly not disappointed when they saw the main attraction of the Sanctuary—the magnificent flock of scarlet Ibis, the country's national bird. They learned that, as if by an inner tugging, these gorgeous winged creatures return every evening at sundown from their feeding grounds to roost in the swampland among the mangrove trees. Joyce and Mandy watched in awe at the mile-long spectacle of those crimson birds in flight against the darkening blue sky.

On Friday, Teasley arrived on time for the trip to the Pitch Lake in the south of the country. They traveled along a well-paved highway that took them through several country districts and villages. They saw rice fields under cultivation that were ploughed by water buffaloes. They also passed cocoa, sugar cane, and citrus plantations en route. They observed laborers walking to the various tracts of land on which they worked, carrying large knives, called cutlasses. Women and children drew water from pipes and springs beyond the villages. With utmost skill, they balanced the buckets of water on top of their heads on pads called "cattas."

Farmers tied their goats, donkeys, and cattle out to graze.

Further along the coastline, they saw fishermen selling their fresh catch to the haggling housewives that besieged them.

"Will you be visiting Tobago while you're here?" Teasley asked them.

"We would have liked to. But we really couldn't fit it into our itinerary," Joyce replied. "We leave on Sunday for Curaçao."

"Tobago. That's Robinson Crusoe's island, isn't it?" Mandy asked.

"So says the folklore," he replied. "But whether it is or not, Tobago is as different from Trinidad as night is from day."

Joyce asked, "How so?"

Teasley explained, "Scarborough, its chief town, is nothing at all like Port of Spain. In fact, the entire island is much more laid-back. It's a lot smaller, is very mountainous, and has many dazzling beaches. Ninety-five percent of the people are of African descent, and very few East Indians live over there.

Mandy reflected, "It seems as if the differences you described are similar to the differences between St. Thomas and St. Croix in the Virgin Islands."

While travelling, Teasley told them that the Pitch Lake to which they were going is the only natural source of asphalt anywhere in the world. Thousands of tons are exported annually to pave roads and highways the world over. They soon discovered that it is indeed a fascinating natural wonder of the world. However, Mandy was rather disappointed when she actually saw the Lake.

"It's not very exciting to look at, is it?" she observed, looking over the grayish-black substance.

Mandy also remarked on the strong odor of sulphur that she smelled coming from the Lake.

However, her interest heightened when she realized that they could actually walk over or even drive over the one hundred acres of it!

Teasley had mentioned, "There's been a never-ending supply of it for centuries. Its true source is still a mystery, but it's estimated to be nearly three hundred feet deep, and it bubbles up continuously."

Later that afternoon on the return trip to Arima, Joyce ventured, "Trinidad is alleged to be the richest nation in the Caribbean, isn't it?"

Teasley replied, a wee bit defensively, "Tourism brings in the dollars in other islands. In Trinidad, oil is king. By the way, our oil fields are only a few miles south of here."

"Is the oil refined here also?" asked Mandy.

"One of the largest refineries in the Commonwealth is located here," he proudly announced. "Several petroleum companies operate, making it one of our most valuable industries."

The wedding on Saturday was simply gorgeous. It was a medium-sized affair and drew about one hundred guests from a wide cross-section of Trinidadian society. The ceremony took place in a well-known church in Port of Spain. Mandy and Joyce donned the best of their finery, while Angela wore a beautiful traditional Indian sari. She explained to Joyce and Mandy how it was made and which accessories she had chosen to go with it. A burgundy-colored sleeveless cotton blouse ended at her midriff and is called a choli. The magenta and gold silk sari comprised six yards of fabric that had been imported from India. It was overlaid in hand-embroidered gold threadwork. Sequins were arranged in intricate patterns of tiny stars and flowers in the fabric. The garment was long and flowing with a number of pleats at the center. It was draped diagonally across her left shoulder.

"I love your jewelry!" Mandy exclaimed when she saw the ornate gold pieces that Angela wore.

She was bedecked in long-hanging filigree earrings called "jhunkas." Around her neck was a large, heavy necklace called a "tilari." She wore handsome slippers on her feet, called "chappals."

In the center of her forehead she'd placed a red beauty mark, called a bindi, which added to her attractiveness.

Oudit arrived early to escort them. He was tastefully dressed in western attire. His tailored three-piece suit was cut in the latest style. It was navy blue with tapered trousers overlaid with herringbone stitching.

The artfully-decorated church reminded Mandy of a tropical garden. Ginger lilies, daisies, and orchids covered a temporary arch that was set up in front of the altar. Flowers were also attached to the sides of each pew. She spotted Teasley and Daisy as they were being ushered to seats near the front. They smiled slightly as they passed Mandy's pew.

Sandra, the bride, was radiant in a full-length gown of peau de soie and guipuire lace with detachable train. Its sleeves and bodice were overlaid with tulle netting, as was the three-tiered veil of her headwear. She carried a lovely, cascading bouquet of fresh white anthuriums. A spray of rust-orange tea roses was intermingled into it.

Charles, the bridegroom, wore a traditional cream colored tuxedo. He and his bride were a striking pair. Mandy listened carefully as they said their vows and noted to herself how happy they seemed. When the lovely ceremony was over, their reception was held at a hillside hotel on the outskirts of the city. After champagne toasting and the traditional speeches were made, a full-course meal was served. Friends and family then joined them in dancing, wishing them much happiness in their new life together.

Mandy lamented to Angela's parents as she and Joyce prepared to leave the island on Sunday, "This winds up our stay in your beautiful country."

"Too bad you won't be around for carnival, Mandy. Unless, of course, you come again in a few months' time," Mrs. Singh declared. "Trinidad is the cradle of steel band and calypso in the West Indies, you know."

"We sampled it in Antigua not long ago," she replied. "It was a grand celebration, but I've heard that Trinidad's carnival beats them all."

"Try to come in February the next time, then. You'll always be welcomed to stay with us."

"I'll be in Barbados next month, Joyce," Angela advised, as they drove to the airport. "I'll be attending a meeting there and was wondering if you'll be back home in Barbados by then."

"Oh yes. Curaçao is our next stop and is the final leg of our tour. By this time next week it will be all over. Lord willing, Mandy will have winged her way back north and I'll have returned home to savor the last few days of my vacation."

"You'll love Curaçao," Angela assured them as they hugged and parted. "Get ready to practice your Dutch, ladies, it's a charming little corner of Holland."

CHAPTER 11

Curios Of Curaçao

"**I** can't believe that this is our final destination, Aunt Joyce," said Mandy, nostalgically, as they crossed the pontoon bridge. "Although we've covered hundreds of miles since we started, it seems like only yesterday that we were flying south from Miami."

"All good things must eventually come to an end," Joyce wistfully replied. "I'm certain that the memories of this journey will stay with us for a long time, though."

The day before, they had flown to this picturesque island of Curaçao. They were both strangers to this charming Dutch territory, sitting thirty-eight miles off the coast of Venezuela.

Mandy declared, "After all of the fun and good times that we've had with so many friends, it seems odd to find ourselves in a place where we know absolutely no one."

"That's what makes it exciting! It's a wonderful way to completely unwind," Joyce said.

Their hotel manager had provided them with a packet of information on Curaçao when they checked in. Included was a booklet providing a brief history of the island. Mandy read that Curaçao is the "C" in the so-called "A-B-C Islands." The booklet explained that this island, along with Aruba and Bonaire, are three of the six islands that comprise the Netherlands Antilles. Aruba is oil-rich and refines oil imported from Venezuela. It's located fifty miles west of Curaçao. Bonaire's most famous attraction is its gorgeous pink flamingoes that nest on the salt ponds there by the thousands. Tons of salt, a major product, are exported annually from there.

Mandy continued reading and discovered that the other three Dutch West Indian islands are located far north of the A-B-Cs. Saba, Sint Maarten, and St. Eustatius are nestled among the English-speaking windward islands. As is true of the A-B-Cs, the inhabitants are Dutch citizens.

That day, as Mandy and Joyce set out to sightsee in the quaint, sprawling capital, Willemstad, they felt as if they'd been transported to Amsterdam in Holland. They heard the Dutch language spoken for the first time and exchanged their dollars for guilders. They observed that the buildings along the waterfront as well as the surrounding houses are a kaleidoscope of pastel colors—their soothing shades ranging from primrose pink to apricot, amber, beige, lilac, turquoise, and olive green. Their architectural designs are typical of those of the Netherlands. They are rectangular-shaped with steep roofs, and most are three stories high. Mandy observed that the streets are squeaky clean and proudly have names such as Heerenstraat, Breedestraat, and Prinsenstraat.

They found the pontoon bridge an attraction in itself. It caters only to pedestrians and swings open several times per day to enable ocean-bound vessels to pass through Sint Annabaai, a harbor channel there. The bridge also divides the city in two, with one section called Punda, meaning "point," and the other section called Otra Banda, literally meaning "the other side."

They noted that Punda is very commercial and contains a complex of shopping malls. By contrast, Otra Banda is largely residential.

After browsing a while and having lunch in Punda, they hired a taxi to take them to and from Otra Banda. Mandy was anxious to visit the famous Curaçao Museum.

They reached Otra Banda via the modern and spectacular Queen Juliana Bridge, which has a four-lane highway and ferries vehicular traffic to the other side.

When they arrived at the museum, they noticed that it was surrounded by a lovely garden. It was quite attractive, despite the fact that the island is flat and arid with little vegetation.

The museum is housed in a nineteenth-century great house, which at one time had served as a military hospital.

The artifacts on display took visitors back through the island's history. There were samples of petroglyphs, or rock carvings, from the original Arawak Indians, who, centuries before, had inhabited the island. They saw relics from the days of sixteenth-century Spanish conquistadors. Items preserved from seventeenth-century plantation days were also viewed. Mandy also learned that when the Dutch seized Curaçao during that time, it became a trading center for slaves from Africa's West Coast.

The biggest surprise to learn about concerned Peter Stuyvesant, the one-legged Dutch governor of New York, then called New Amsterdam, back in the 1600s. Mandy had studied about him in school. She found out during this museum visit that he had been once in charge of Curaçao!

"What are you two doing here?" Joyce exclaimed as they exited the museum.

Pat and Oliver Downes, friends of Joyce's who lived in Aruba, were entering the museum.

"We took the short hop over here for a couple of days' vacation," Pat informed. "We're having a great time."

"We're leaving the day after tomorrow," Joyce told them. "This is the last leg of an indescribable tour."

"If you don't have anything planned for this evening, will you join us at our hotel for dinner?" Oliver invited.

They eagerly accepted and were soon on their way.

"Pat and Oliver were neighbors of mine when I moved to Barbados," Joyce explained. "Oliver works for a telecommunications company and recently was sent to manage its Aruba operations."

Returning to Punda, Joyce and Mandy continued their shopping expedition on foot. They sampled the wares in the marvelous eighteen-block shopping emporium. As they promenaded through the "pedestrians-only" mall, they couldn't believe the rock bottom prices of several luxury items. There were exquisite French perfumes, fragile china pieces, Swedish crystal, and jewelry of every description on sale. Other stores sold sportswear, luggage, cameras, Thai and Indian fabrics, and a host of other commodities from Holland. Mandy was impressed by the dress shops in several streets. Elegant garments caught her eye in the windows of fashionable ladies' salons.

"Has your cash run out yet?" Joyce asked her, as she cast a wistful eye herself.

Laughing, Mandy, replied, "It's a lucky thing I'm heading home this week, or you'd have to bail me out."

They meandered to the northern end of the shopping center to view Willemstad's famous floating market. They couldn't leave Curaçao without seeing it. Schooners from nearby South America had pulled into Waaigat, the harbor inlet. They had dropped anchor and slanted their sails to provide shade for the produce on sale. It was fascinating to watch the mountains of fresh vegetables, fruit, and fish, literally, moving up and down, as the boats tilted in rhythm with the water. Shopping at this market, they learned, was a long tradition in Curaçao.

Oliver and Pat were staying at one of the city's fine luxury hotels. As Joyce and Mandy entered, they immediately sensed the sophisticated, though congenial, atmosphere. The main concourse was a beehive of activity as guests and visitors mingled. Ladies clad in the latest fashions moved through the front lobby. Immaculately-uniformed bellboys scurried around, transporting luggage to and from the various guests' rooms. Joyce asked a receptionist to let the Downeses know they'd arrived.

As they waited, Mandy glanced at a hotel directory. Listed at ground-level locations off various points in the lobby were a shopping arcade, a casino, a disco and nightclub, tennis courts, and a steam bath and sauna.

"This hotel seems to have every kind of service available for its guests," she said.

There were four different eating establishments on the premises—a small café for quick meals and snacks, a posh skyline restaurant for elegant intimate occasions, a main dining room that offered fine international cuisine, and, finally, a huge banquet hall that accommodated large social affairs. Their hosts had made reservations in the main dining room.

"Masha danki," Mandy said slowly to the waiter as he handed her a long, elaborate menu.

He flashed her a full, warm smile, realizing that she'd learned a few words of Papiamento since she arrived there.

She was told that it's the historic and colorful language of the A-B-C islands. Passed on from parents to children, this language, both written and spoken, is a lovely combination of Arawak Indian, Spanish, Dutch, Portuguese, French, and African dialects, with a few English words mixed in.

Oliver provided some more information about this comparatively new language in the world.

"As the various immigrants and colonizers arrived over a three-hundred-year period, they needed a common tongue to help them communicate with each other. Each group added its own smattering of phrases, but the Spanish contributed about sixty percent."

"Even certain works by Shakespeare have been translated into Papiamento," Pat injected. "Novels and newspapers are printed in this expressive language here in Curaçao and also in Aruba."

"What's it like to live in Aruba?" Joyce asked them. "Is it anything like Curaçao?"

Oliver had been a history major when he attended the university. He had also read extensively about these islands before they moved to Aruba.

He replied, "Curaçao is the center of government for the Netherlands Antilles. Therefore, as you'd expect, many more official and commercial activities take place here. However, tourism is growing fast as an industry in Aruba, especially because of our beautiful beaches."

"Is Aruba as dry as Curaçao?" Mandy questioned.

"All of the A-B-Cs are dry, with cacti of many varieties and divi-divi trees growing everywhere."

"Would you tell us about the places that you've been to on your tour?" Pat asked. "We'd love to hear about them."

In turn, Mandy and Joyce shared with their friends a few of their many adventures.

"Which of the islands would you choose to visit again, Mandy?" asked Oliver.

"I'd really have to think about that," Mandy said. "Each one is so different and has something so unique to offer."

"You'll probably be able to decide which one you enjoyed best after you get home," Joyce declared. "You'll be able to reflect better on why one was more appealing to you than the other."

After dinner, they stayed for the evening entertainment and then returned to their hotel, a small, quiet inn on the outskirts of Punda.

Joyce and Mandy ordered room service for breakfast and spent their final day on the beach.

"Don't feel so downhearted, Mandy," her aunt encouraged. "The Caribbean is like a magnet. Once you've come on your first visit, you keep coming back for more."

White sandy beaches fringed by sturdy coconut palms
breathe tranquility on the West Indian islands.
Photo by the Author, Dallas, Texas

CHAPTER 12

Farewell

Joyce and Mandy reminisced at length on their final day about their memorable expedition through the sun-dappled islands of the Caribbean. They were certain that no other folks in the world had experienced anything quite like it.

"When we started in Miami," Joyce reflected, laughing, "you were a bundle of nerves underneath your calm exterior, not knowing what to expect."

"I feel so different now, Aunt Joyce," she replied. "I feel ready to travel anywhere in the world."

"I left a copy of our itinerary with Dot and Jean in Nassau," said Joyce. "I'm sure they've been following our movements step by step."

Mandy reflected, "I wonder what Billie is up to over in Haiti? I'll be sure to drop her a line and also write the St. Jacqueses when I get back home."

"Don't forget about your pals, Louis, Sam, and Lena in Jamaica," Joyce reminded her.

"How could I ever forget our unbelievable day in Ocho Rios? The climb up the Dunn's River Falls was breathtaking. I really would like to visit there again. I'd also make sure to visit Montego Bay and other places in Jamaica that we didn't get to on this trip," said Mandy.

"I know you're looking forward to having Lisa Christian visit you in New York next summer. No lost handbags on the subways, please! Knowing New York, I'm afraid you won't be as lucky to find it as you were in St. Thomas," remarked Joyce.

On and on they recounted the high points of their tour through each location—from the eerie "Baths" in Virgin Gorda to the rollicking carnival in Antigua. They shuddered, remembering their frightening hurricane experience in Dominica and relished again the Indian feasts in Trinidad.

"We've kidded many times about writing a book about this trip, Aunt Joyce. But I seriously want to give it a try. I know for sure that my school assignments in the coming year will be loaded with my experiences."

"Don't lay it on too thickly, young lady. You'll make your friends and teachers green with envy. Give them just enough to whet their appetites. Make them want to come, themselves."

Mandy and Joyce fell silent as they drove through Curaçao's beautiful countryside on the way to the airport. After a loving embrace, they parted, each taking her separate flight home. Joyce took a regional airline and departed for Barbados, while Mandy boarded a big Dutch aircraft for her non-stop flight to New York.

When she landed in New York, Mandy felt a fresh new bounce in her step. She knew at that moment that those Caribbean Islands had etched a new place in heart.

Epilogue

After many years, Amanda is keeping her promise to continue the Caribbean adventure that she started long ago. Her upcoming vacation aboard a luxury cruise liner with her husband and three children, will take them to most of the places that she visited before. Although she knows that, no doubt, so much has changed, she's still anxious to recapture some of her memorable experiences and introduce her family to them. She's certain that a lot has still remained the same.

Aunt Joyce, her feisty traveling companion of long ago, is now retired from her job with the airlines. However, she's still living in Barbados with her husband, Keith. Amanda can't wait to see them again after such a long time.

There are only two weeks left to get ready for the cruise. Amanda's heart skips a beat in anticipation. So, once again, all aboard!

27164149R00102

Made in the USA
Charleston, SC
03 March 2014